"Five, six, seven, eight, walk left, right, together and turn."

Fanny's voice moved in the same rhythm as her body, and it made it easier for even a graceless oaf like Law to follow along as he untwisted his body toward hers, his hand continuing to grasp her tightly.

"All right." She cleared her throat. "Now we'll put the whole thing together with music and then record."

"Oh right." For a second, Law had forgotten they were doing this for another couple. When she was in his arms, it felt like the rest of the world melted away. "Yes, I'm ready. To, um, record."

Because as much as he liked the image of him and Fanny dancing together at a wedding, he still wasn't ready for forever. But something in him whispered that the longer he spent with Fanny, the harder it would be to imagine himself with anyone else as his partner. On the dance floor and in life.

Dear Reader,

In my forty-mumble-mumble years on this planet, I've learned a lot.

One of my biggest takeaways is that life rarely goes the way you plan and almost everything is entirely out of your control. When faced with roadblocks to their dreams, some people will try to go around them, moving on to the next journey too quickly to realize that a little patience and persistence can sometimes get them exactly where they wanted to be. Others will be so immobilized they can't move at all, finding themselves stuck between the past that no longer exists and a future they can't yet envision.

In *Their First Dance*, both main characters have physical injuries that prevent them from achieving all they wanted to do. As a former dancer, Fanny is used to not accepting anything less than perfection, while Lawson's coping mechanism as a woodworker is typically to toss mistakes away and start over with a fresh block of wood. Even though neither believes in fate, the magic that is Crystal Hill brings them together to learn from each other's very different perspectives...and also reminds them that love is always worth putting in the work.

Happy reading!

Laurie

THEIR FIRST DANCE

LAURIE BATZEL

Harlequin
HEARTWARMING

If you purchased this book without a cover you should be aware that this book is stolen property. It was reported as "unsold and destroyed" to the publisher, and neither the author nor the publisher has received any payment for this "stripped book."

Harlequin®
HEARTWARMING™

ISBN-13: 978-1-335-46011-0

Their First Dance

Copyright © 2025 by Laurie Batzel

All rights reserved. No part of this book may be used or reproduced in any manner whatsoever without written permission.

Without limiting the author's and publisher's exclusive rights, any unauthorized use of this publication to train generative artificial intelligence (AI) technologies is expressly prohibited.

This is a work of fiction. Names, characters, places and incidents are either the product of the author's imagination or are used fictitiously. Any resemblance to actual persons, living or dead, businesses, companies, events or locales is entirely coincidental.

For questions and comments about the quality of this book, please contact us at CustomerService@Harlequin.com.

TM and ® are trademarks of Harlequin Enterprises ULC.

Harlequin Enterprises ULC
22 Adelaide St. West, 41st Floor
Toronto, Ontario M5H 4E3, Canada
www.Harlequin.com

Printed in U.S.A.

Laurie Batzel lives in the Poconos with her husband, their four two-legged children and their two four-legged children, Stuart the Corgi and Midge the Marvelous Rescue Pup. Her first book, *With My Soul*, was published in 2019, and her essays can be found in several editions of *Chicken Soup for the Soul*, as well as online at *McSweeney's Internet Tendency*, *Longreads* and Harvard University's *Tuesday Magazine*. When not writing romance that is equal parts swoons, sniffles and smiles, she can be found watching too much TV under too many blankets, testing the acceptable limits of caffeine consumption and perfecting her recipe for chocolate chip cookies. Learn more at *authorlauriebatzel.com*.

Also by Laurie Batzel

Harlequin Heartwarming

A Crystal Hill Romance

The Dairy Queen's Second Chance
The Valentine Plan
The Teacher's Forever Family

Visit the Author Profile page at Harlequin.com.

To my early dance teachers who taught me so much more than pliés and pirouettes: Gigi Rousseau, Marianne Godfrey and the late Arnott Mader, whose predilection for giving all his students nicknames inspired that particular Crystal Hill quirk.

He called me The General, and an attempt to revive that moniker within my own family was politely declined by all after they had stopped laughing and pointing at me.

Acknowledgments

Eternal thanks to...

My family: My husband, James, and my kids, Charles, Cameron, Cody and Caroline. You are all my inspiration, my heart and my home.

My agent, Stacey Graham, and Three Seas Literary: Thank you for going along this journey with me. Onward!

The team at Harlequin Heartwarming, especially Johanna Raisanen and Kathleen Scheibling, I am so grateful for your enthusiastic support and insightful direction. Also a special thank-you to the other amazing Harlequin Heartwarming authors whose books I love and whose company I was so privileged to enjoy at Harlequin's 75th Anniversary Gala last year in Toronto!

My parents, in-laws and extended family, thank you for all your support and encouragement.

Finally, and always, to CJ: thanks for today.

CHAPTER ONE

THE MORE STONES Lawson Carl laid out for the foundation of his house, the more he believed the theory that it was actually aliens who built the Great Pyramids of Egypt.

He'd just finished the footprint of the floor plan and needed to take a water break. It wasn't even a very big floor plan. There was space enough for two bedrooms—one for him and one for guests, mainly his parents who had moved to South Carolina a year ago. There was also an open-concept living room and kitchen. The kitchen had scope for him to display the custom cheese boards he made and sold in his online shop along with wooden sculptures, custom shelves and pretty much anything else you could make from a block of wood.

Well, the things he used to make before the accident in his woodshop. It had been almost six months and his right arm that had suffered the crush injury still wasn't fully recovered. He'd done a few weeks of physical therapy, and while it had helped with the initial pain, he didn't have the same strength and dexterity as before. So now, instead of working on the fine carvings that had been bringing in a decent living for over a year since he moved back to his hometown of Crystal Hill, he was advertising his services online as a "handyman," including painting and staining decks, power-washing homes, and simple furniture refacing and repairs. Eventually, he would need to figure out a long-term plan, but the beauty of being thirty-two and single with no kids was that there was no pressure to figure anything out immediately. Something would come along and move him in the right direction. It always did.

So, for now, he distracted himself with rearranging pavers in different floor plans on the land his parents had gifted him before they moved. It had come with a trailer, which was where he was living at the moment and was conveniently adjacent to his cousin BeeBee's dairy farm for those days he didn't feel like driving into town for a gallon of milk. However, with his carpentry career running aground and his love life at a lull, he needed to make progress on *something* in his life.

Hence, pavers and rotating house plans.

His phone buzzed. Still crouching in the spot where he had laid the last paver, he pulled it out of the back pocket of his jeans and checked to see who had called him. It was Mrs. Habervent, one of his octogenarian clients who frequently called him for tech support.

"Handyman Law, what's your trouble?" he answered with his standard line. "Mmm-hmm. Yup, I see. So, what you want to do is click on the box that says 'Select multiple' in the top right corner. See it? No, not that—there you go. Okay, now you should be able to add multiple pictures to your Facebook post. And remember, if you see a post that reads 'Can't believe he's really dead,' with a link below it, don't click on the link. That's right, no one's really died; it's a scam. Payment?" Usually, his clients paid with an app like Venmo or Zelle, but Mrs. Habervent wasn't ready for that anytime soon. "No need, Mrs. H. This one's on the house. Okay, bye now."

He hung up quickly before she offered her granddaughter's phone number as payment. Again. All previous efforts to explain why that wasn't okay on multiple levels had gone ignored, so he opted for the path of least resistance. Even worse, she wasn't the only one of his clients to do it. He had been away from this goofy, lovable town for so long, he had forgotten how intense people here got about finding their happily-ever-after...and once they found it for themselves, finding it for their neighbors quickly became their next quest. Even his parents had tried it last year by pitting him and his brother Lucas against each other for the apartment behind the family cheese and dairy shop Lucas ran. The winner of the space would be the brother who got engaged first—a nod to their parents' long-standing concerns about both brothers' commitment issues. It had almost worked and Law had gone through several old contacts in his phone before he had seen Lucas with a woman who had just arrived in town to start a cheese-board party hosting business. He had never seen his sober, cheese-obsessed brother so utterly besotted. Almost instantly, Law had stopped pursuing the space and the other women in town and began working behind the scenes to get Lucas out of his own way. It had worked, and now Lucas and his wife, Chrysta, were the proud parents of baby Rosabell—Bell for short—and Law got the trailer, the land, and the title of fun uncle, so it was a win all the way around.

Law pushed his hands off his knees and groaned as the muscles in his back screamed. The accident in his woodshop had really messed him up. He had spent his twenties working as a rock climbing guide, a semi-pro snowboarder and, once, even a jousting knight at a traveling Renaissance Faire, but now he couldn't even stand up without letting out an old-man groan. Between his failing body, the town's matchmaking efforts and the pang in his heart when he watched Lucas and Chrysta communicate telepathically over their baby's head, sometimes it felt like the Universe was pushing him to finally settle down in one place, with one woman. A part of him liked the idea. It was probably the same part of him that thrilled whenever he babysat his niece and she fell asleep on his lap while watching her cartoons. At the same time, he had grown up with most of the women in town, and as captain of the hockey team and lead vocalist in a popular local band, had been popular enough to go on his share of dates. But none of those women soothed the other part of him, the restless voyager who longed to forge new paths in the wilderness and carve shapes and designs from plain blocks of wood. No, he was still very much enjoying his days as the itinerant town handyman and fun uncle. There would be plenty of time for settling down in the distant someday.

Another alarm went off on his phone, this one

a tinkling fairylike bell from *The Nutcracker*. Time to take his cousin Georgia's daughter, Caroline, to her dance class. He wasn't technically fun uncle to Caroline, but as she had no real uncles, he was happy to step into the role. Caroline's dad had passed away over five years ago and her mom was now dating Caroline's third-grade teacher, Malcolm Gulleson. The two were working on opening up a quartz mining site in the woods next to his property, and since Law was close, it was easy to pick Caroline up. He stepped back and surveyed the building blocks of his single-floor castle.

Yup. It was good to be king.

He brushed off his hands and made his way to his Jeep. Driving on the main road, he met Georgia, Malcolm and Caroline at the cleared entrance into the woods. Law pulled over and slowed to a stop.

Georgia opened the passenger side-door for Caroline and helped her inside. "Have fun at dance class, sweetheart," she said, tightening her daughter's seat belt, then leaned to one side to nod at Law. "Thank you so much for doing this. The health inspector is coming to look over the concessions area, so I really needed to be here to show him around."

"Once word gets out that Georgia's Bakery,

winner of the Food Network Regional Baking Competition, is supplying the eats, this place is going to be a hit," Law said. He raised a hand to Malcolm, who wiped his forehead with the back of his arm before returning the gesture. "You're going to be serving your giant chocolate chip cookies here, right?"

"Of course," Georgia said proudly. Her bakery downtown was a favorite with both the locals and the Manhattanites who descended on the town every summer. After Georgia won the Food Network contest and appeared on a popular show on the channel, people were coming to the town from all over to visit the bakery. It was a boon to a lot of the local businesses, especially his brother's cheese shop and the cheese board-building party events Chrysta hosted in the back. Lawson had been making decent money off the cheese boards he made for them until the accident. He had tried getting back into it by offering to supply the basic cheese boards for her Christmas cheese board party demonstration, but the process had been painful and extremely time-consuming due to the nerve damage in his wrist. After that, he had given up entirely and focused his energy on the handyman business. What was the point in continuing to do something that hurt you?

"Shiny rocks and big cookies?" He winked at Caroline. "That's a kid's idea of paradise right there. Heck, that's my idea of paradise too and I'm a grown man."

"Only on the outside." Georgia shook her head, her shoulder-length curls brushing her cheeks with the motion. "On the inside, you're still the same kid who convinced my mom to put his marshmallow and grape jelly peanut butter cookie sandwich creations in the display case at the bakery for a week."

"They sold like gangbusters, though, didn't they?"

"I'm pretty sure ninety percent of the orders came from you, but yes, they were a hit, and no, I'm not bringing them back," Georgia shot back, laughing. "Everyone has to grow up sometime, Law, even you."

Law stuck out his tongue in response. "I won't and you can't make me. Growing up is for suckers, right, C-dog?" He elbowed Caroline, who threw her head back against the seat of the Jeep and giggled.

"Laugh all you want," Georgia admonished him. "One of these days you're going to meet a woman who makes you want to give up the Lost Boy life for good."

"Well, unless she's hiding behind one of Malcolm's rocks back there—" he pointed at the forest "—I don't see her showing up in this small town any time soon. Now if you'll excuse me, Care Bear and I are needed at the dance studio."

"I'm sorry, you're going to dance classes now?" Georgia asked.

Law wasn't offended by her incredulity. Most things in life had come easily to him: hockey, singing, climbing, woodworking, pretty much anything that required a little physical strength and the energy he had in abundance. But dancing had always been the one thing that he had never been able to master or charm his way into faking. Even when he was voted homecoming and prom king, he had simply foisted the royal dance onto the more nimble members of the court. His running joke as a snowboarding instructor had always been that he couldn't ski because they didn't make skis for two left feet, so he chose the single board instead.

"Law is helping Madame Rousseau bring up the sets and costumes for the spring recital in May," Caroline chimed in. "She says she's getting too old to carry everything up from the basement anymore."

"All right, have fun, my twinkle toes," Georgia said, waving as she closed the door.

"Right back at you, my sparkle earlobes," he joked as they drove away.

The drive from the edge of the woods into downtown Crystal Hill took them around the lake. The entire town sat comfortably in the shadows of the Adirondack Mountain range of Upstate New York. Winter was only now beginning its annual thaw and everything from the ground to the branches reflected in the lake was brown and wet with melted snow. Yet when Law opened the windows of the Jeep, the smell of promise and new life blew in with the air.

Turning left onto Jane Street, the main drag in Crystal Hill, he pulled over and parked in front of the theater, the letters on the old-timey marquee slightly askew. He typed a note in his phone to ask Madame Rousseau if she wanted the sign fixed or if they planned to leave it that way to add to the local charm.

"C'mon, Carolina Ballerina," he said, opening the passenger door and helping Caroline down from the Jeep. "Your dance space awaits."

The dance studio was next to the theater, a tall narrow building with steep rickety steps leading up to a small door on the left, then more steps to the third floor where the "big girl dancers" had their rehearsals. He opened the door for Caroline and she rushed past to greet the gaggle of other little girls wiggling on a bench in the corridor next to the dance studio. The walls were covered with framed pictures of years and years of past performances, although Law's carpenter's eye went directly to the cracks in the walls hiding behind the pictures and the unevenness of the pressure on the plaster molding in the ceiling corners. This building as well as the theater made up one of the older sections of the street, the dry cleaner, barber and Big Joe's Diner at the end of the block having come along forty years later.

Madame Rousseau emerged from behind a rack of fluffy tutus at the end of the corridor. Leaning heavily on a cane, she jutted a chin up at him. "This place is in worse shape than I am," she said, echoing his thoughts in her thick Queens accent.

"Just needs a little paint and spackle," he said, slapping a hand on the wall and cringing as several hunks of plaster fell to the ground.

"Me or the building?" Madame Rousseau rasped with a chuckle that evolved into a thick cough. Her hands shook as from somewhere within the filmy shawl she wore over her black leotard and skirt she pulled out a peppermint and unwrapped it. "Don't answer that. I think it will take a lot more than paint and spackle for me or the building."

"If you want I'll go around and do a thorough inspection," Law offered, brushing plaster off the shoulder of his T-shirt. "The studio and the theater are Crystal Hill institutions. I'd be happy to help keep them going."

She reached up and patted him on the cheek with a wizened hand. "That's very kind of you, dear. Between you and my sweet Fanny, we might actually be able to get through the spring recital this year without everything collapsing on top of us."

Law blinked twice. On the one hand, Law was all for a woman who was confident in her body and unafraid to celebrate her own, um, assets. On the other hand, he'd been coming to dance recitals and shows for his cousins and female friends since he was ten. Hearing the grandmotherly Madame Rousseau talking about her "sweet Fanny" wasn't something he would ever be prepared to hear.

"Your...um, I'm sorry, what?"

Madame Rousseau gestured with her cane toward the door on the right that Caroline and the other girls were lining along the wall preparing to enter. "See for yourself."

Law pushed the door open cautiously, and

piano music, the same tune that he had set his alarm to, flooded the corridor with its twinkling melody. A group of very young girls who couldn't have been more than four twirled rambunctiously in a circle. At the center of the circle was a dark-haired woman wearing a light purple leotard and a flowy white skirt over tights rolled up above bare ankles. She stood on the very tips of her toes in shiny satin ballet shoes and her arms formed a graceful oval that framed her shoulders and head. As she spun to face the door, her face struck Law breathless. She had pale green eyes, and the violet sparkles on her eyelids made the hue even more magical. A small but full mouth curved up at the corners in an enigmatic smile, and Law found himself thinking there was something almost catlike in her features.

It wasn't just that her looks were striking; the way she moved captivated him instantly. Each finger seemed deliberately placed, the set of her chin and even the way she breathed was in perfect time to the music. Watching her move was like watching the inside of a clock striking the hour. Precision at its finest.

When she lowered her heels to the floor and clasped her hands to her chest, the little girls around her stopped their whirling and gazed up at her as if mesmerized. Law couldn't blame them.

"All right, tiny ballerinas," she said in a hushed voice as she bent her body forward. "Now that we've spun in a circle like a tornado, where have we landed?"

"Disney World!" the chorus of tiny voices chirped and she laughed musically. Straightening her spine in one motion, she put her hands on her hips and shook her head. "It's always Disney World, isn't it? Very well, then. We've arrived at Disney World. So let's get in line for our ride, one after the other. Hands on the shoulders in front of you and make a ballet train for the teacup ride. Choo-choo!"

When she turned in the direction of the door, she leveled him with that icy green gaze. Something flashed in her eyes and her dark eyebrows furrowed slightly. If he didn't know any better he would have thought the expression was hostile, but that couldn't be right. She had to be new in town because he definitely would have remembered a face that gorgeous. that.

Eager to make a good first impression, Law reached his hand out to introduce himself and promptly stubbed his big toe on an uneven floorboard at the doorway. Flying several feet into the dance studio, he landed on his side before rolling onto his back.

"I think you swept me off my feet," he joked, rubbing his hip. That was definitely going to be sore later, but he had a feeling the bruise to his ego was going to be a doozy.

Still laughing, he looked up into the wide-eyed faces of five tiny ballerinas and one beautiful stranger who still did not seem to find him charming at all.

CHAPTER TWO

THE MAN LYING on the dance studio floor at Fanny Cunningham's feet was not a stranger.

Oh, no. She would recognize that face anywhere. First of all, it was a very attractive face. She couldn't deny that, not even to herself. Just as attractive and just as full of unearned confidence in its own charm as it had been the first time she had laid eyes on it over a decade ago.

She cleared her throat and tapped her toes, the hard box of the pointe shoe rendering the sound significantly more intimidating than it would have been in her soft jazz shoes or the bare feet she wore during lyrical classes. "Sir, I'm afraid I'm going to have to ask you to leave the dance studio and come back when you're in proper attire for a ballet class."

He eased onto his feet with a wince that brought Fanny more than a little bit of satisfaction. Brushing off his jeans, he blew a strand of sandy brown hair off his forehead and gave her the wide smile that had taken her in when she was too young to know any better. "Well, uh, I'm afraid I left my tutu at home," he said, striking a pose with his arms flung over his head in what she assumed was an attempt at fifth position of the arms.

The little girls giggled at his antics. Fanny crossed her arms and arched an eyebrow, refusing to be as easily amused as a five-year-old… or a nineteen-year-old girl.

"Fortunately, I always have some extras in the back for situations just like this one," Fanny remarked, turning on her heel and striding across the studio. Digging around in the box of practice tutus the older girls wore for rehearsal, she pulled out one in a particularly garish shade of pink and trotted back to the center of the room. "Here you go." She thrust the bunch of tulle in his hands along with the matching tiara. "But we also don't allow street shoes in the studio. They scuff the floor. If you're going to stay, the sneakers have to go. Socks too."

That should get rid of him. A vain, self-obsessed guy like him would never show his feet. Men's feet were notoriously gross, and as a dancer, she knew a thing or two about how hideous a foot could look.

Yet he slid his feet out of his shoes, then

pulled his socks off before stepping carefully into the tutu and sliding it over his hips. The little girls shrieked with laughter, especially when he began to strike disjointed poses like a marionette with a broken string. He even had the audacity to have nice-looking feet with high arches and clean, well-trimmed toenails. The rudeness, honestly.

He turned and looked over his shoulder at her as he placed the tiara on his head at a rakishly off-kilter angle. "I gotta say, I think this is my color. I could be a model for a bubblegum commercial in this."

"More like Pepto Bismol," Fanny shot back. "Now whenever I see you, I'll think…indigestion."

He pointed a finger gun at her. "But you will see me again?" Spinning back around, he put his hands on his hips, looked down then back up at her with earnestness that had to have been well-rehearsed. "In all seriousness, I don't believe we've been properly introduced. I'm Lawson Carl. And you are…?"

Fanny's jaw actually fell open. He didn't remember her. It had been a long time ago and they had only spent a few hours together, but still. Now she wished she had given him the pink fairy wand that went with the tutu and tiara. And then poked him in the eye with it.

One of her students chimed in for her. "This is Miss Fanny. She's our dance teacher."

A look of dawning comprehension brightened his features. "You're Fanny," he said with a strangely relieved chuckle. "Thank goodness. For a minute there, I was afraid Madame Rousseau was trying to pull a Mrs. Robinson on me."

Fanny cocked her head to the side. "Do you really think you're that irresistible to all women?"

"No, it's not—it was something she said." He held up his hands and shook his head. "Look, can we start over? Fanny, that's gotta be a nickname or short for something."

Fanny pointed to the door. "Mr. Carl, you've had your fun, but these girls need to curtsy before they finish class. If you don't mind…"

He fake-pouted. "Fine. I'll leave while I still have my dignity intact."

Sticking his chin in the air, he pivoted sharply and made for the door, swinging his hips in an exaggerated fashion.

Fanny bit back a smile, refusing to even give his back the satisfaction of knowing that he amused her. "Mr. Carl?"

He whipped around, a hopeful light in his sky blue eyes. "Yes?"

She held out her hand. "My tutu please."

"Oh, right." He walked back and shimmied ungracefully out of the stiff skirt and handed it back to her. "Here you go." He started to turn again, but she interrupted his exit.

"And the tiara."

With a wounded sigh of martyrdom even Joan of Arc would have found excessively maudlin, he pulled the tiara off his head and gave it to her. Plodding toward the door with his chin to his chest, he muttered loud enough for everyone to hear. "Now I don't feel like a pretty princess anymore."

The real grace note to the whole performance came when he got to the loose floorboard at the doorway and remembered that he had stubbed his toe. Suddenly lifting his foot like a golden doodle attempting to wheedle an extra sausage at a picnic, he hobbled toward the corridor, bending down to pick up his shoes and socks before he left the room.

Only when he was completely out of sight did Fanny allow the grin she had been fighting the whole time to finally break free and spread across her face. She clapped her hands. "Enough shenanigans, ladies. Now that it's just us serious artists, are we doing our final curtsy to 'Baby Shark' or the theme song from *Bluey*?"

Once the tiny ballerinas had filed out, the nine- and ten-year-olds began to line up at the barre followed by Madame Rousseau. Fanny's heart ached at the way her mentor's ramrod straight spine had started to hunch forward. Her illness last year must have taken a serious toll, one that continued as Madame Rousseau launched into another fit of deep, painful coughs before leaning on the piano and raising her chin to Fanny.

"I just wanted to say again how grateful I am that you came back to help out this spring," she rasped. "I never would have managed without your help."

"Well, it was good timing," Fanny remarked. "The surgeon had just cleared the last of the weight-bearing restrictions when you called." She couldn't keep the bitterness out of her voice. As if there was anything good about a fall onstage in the middle of a performance that resulted in a tear to the labrum, the lining of the hip joint, so severe that it required surgical intervention. Once the doctors had gone in, they found the cartilage so degenerated after years of dance training that she had required a partial hip replacement. Being the youngest patient in the physical therapy unit by several decades had been awkward. Having her performing career end at least ten years earlier than she had planned and so abruptly that she didn't even finish her last performance? Well, that was a wound no amount of physical therapy could heal.

Madame Rousseau made a tutting noise. "I was so sorry to hear about your injury. Following your career has been one of my most rewarding experiences as a teacher. Not many people can transition from the classical ballet world to working on multiple Broadway shows."

Fanny sighed as she bent down to pick up a stray bobby pin that had popped out of one of the little girls' buns. "Ironically, I made the switch thinking it would help extend my career. You know as well as I do ballet dancers rarely keep working past late thirties, but Broadway hoofers can keep going into their forties if they're lucky." She stood up and shook her head. "Great planning, huh?"

To be fair, it wasn't her plan that had been the problem. After all, it certainly hadn't been her plan to get paired up with a dancer who was ninety percent ego and at least five percent perfectly coiffed hair. All it had taken was one errant strand of the long locks the hair and makeup department had warned him repeatedly about tying back more securely because they feared it would get in his face and impede his vision. Which, of course, it did—during a lift, no less—and when he instinctively moved his hand to brush it away, down she had gone. She didn't want revenge. She just wanted to have the chance to end an amazing career on a higher note. Literally, as she had come crashing down next to the male lead right as he hit a spectacularly low bass note during the run of *Carousel*.

A chorus of female laughter pealed outside the door. Madame Rousseau leaned back to peer at the source of the revelry, then looked back at Fanny with a knowing smile. "Mr. Carl has been helping me clear out the costume storage in the back. He's quite the character. Did you meet him?"

"More than once," Fanny commented wryly. "The last time was when I came to town to guest-star here in *The Nutcracker*. Remember?"

"You were the most beautiful Sugarplum Fairy," Madame Rousseau said. "That was when Law's cousin, Lindsay Long, was Clara. He must have been there to support her. The Longs and the Carls have always been more like siblings to each other than cousins. I didn't realize you two had run into each other."

"Almost literally," Fanny said. Law had been tasked with delivering a giant bouquet of flowers to his younger cousin and had his vision obscured by a particularly resplendent peony. He had collided with Fanny as she was leaving the stage after the final bows. This time, she had been the one to fall at his feet. When the flower petals and leftover fake snow had settled, she had looked up into an incredibly handsome face with guilt and concern mingling into an adorable, puppyish expression. He was more than just cute, he was daytime-soap-opera-star cute and when he offered his hand to help her up, electricity had shot through her entire body at the first touch. Looking back, she knew that was only because she was not even twenty, the age when hormones and delusions about knights in shining armor transformed any casual contact into a potential thrill ride. She certainly knew better now than to fall for a guy like that, so good-looking and clearly aware of it. Even his self-deprecating joke about having two left feet had a touch of arrogance, as if he knew even then he didn't need to be coordinated.

They had flirted shamelessly backstage for several minutes and the fact that he left her side only to congratulate his younger cousin had fooled her into thinking this was the unicorn of guys—sweet, family-oriented and willing to sit through an entire production of *The*

Nutcracker without complaining about missing some sports event. He had returned swiftly with a single rose he had pilfered from the arrangement and offered it to her. The kill shot had been when he complimented her on the fouetté turns in the finale and told her that her classical line reminded him of a young Darci Kistler. Her eyes had practically popped out of her head until he sheepishly confessed that while he was gone he had asked his cousin for some technical jargon to impress her. The deception had come off as disarmingly humorous to a younger Fanny who, being a trusting idiot, had agreed to go with him for a post-show root beer float at the local diner.

They had just started on their float—they shared one with two straws, like in the movies—when an irate girl whom Fanny recognized as one of the rose dancers in "Waltz of the Flowers" came up to their table, irate and crying hysterically.

"We've been going out for the last three weeks," she had sobbed. The girl's stage makeup had run down her face in black mascara tracks, making the moment even more uncomfortable because Fanny really wanted to offer her a napkin for her face, but under the circumstances figured it would be unhelpful. "Did that mean nothing to you?"

"Bonnie, I never said we were exclusive." He at least had the decency to look thoroughly chagrined, although whether it was due to his actions or the eyes of half of the families who had been in attendance at the performance staring at them she would never know.

This provoked a fresh shower of tears, out of which Fanny could barely make out the words, "Bonnie? Who's Bonnie? My name is Bailey, you jerk."

And with that, she had run back to her family's booth in the corner.

Fanny had leveled Law with a shocked stare. "Seriously? You're just going to sit there?"

He had shrugged. "Like I said, we never talked about not seeing other people. It's not my fault she got attached." Leaning forward on his elbows, he jutted his chin at Fanny. "Besides, once I saw you, it was like no one else in the world existed."

Fanny had matched his pose, resting her elbows on the table with her fingers a breath away from his. "And what's *my* name?"

His eyes had widened while his mouth opened and closed like a fish gasping for water. "I—uh, well, we just met, remember? Give me a second."

She stood up, her chair screeching loudly enough for everyone in the diner to turn around and stare at them once more, but she didn't care. "That's what I thought. I don't have time for boys who play around with girls' feelings. I spend twelve hours a day in class, rehearsals or performing. If someone wants to be with me, they need to be in it for real. Call me when you grow up."

She made her way to the glass door and his voice followed her. "But I don't have your number."

Looking over her shoulder, she smiled at him. "You catch on quick, lover boy. Maybe you're not just a pretty face after all."

She recounted the story to Madame Rousseau, who seemed surprisingly unfazed. "To be fair, everyone in town knew Law was a huge flirt back then. Bailey got back together with her ex-boyfriend shortly after that and now they're married and living in Scranton with three beautiful children, so it all worked out."

"How can you defend him?" Fanny shook her head. "There's no excuse for guys who think they get a free pass on fidelity just because they're good-looking." Really good-looking, but that was beside the point. "If I'm with someone, then I need to know they're as passionate and committed to the relationship as I am with everything in my life. You don't make it as a dancer unless you give one hundred and fifty percent every class, every rehearsal. It's the same thing in love."

Madame Rousseau cleared her throat, raising painted-on auburn eyebrows at Fanny. "And how has this all-or-nothing philosophy fared in your love life recently?"

Fanny avoided her eyes. She walked to the corner by the barre where cubes of rosin lay in a small wooden box for dancers to rub on the soles of their shoes to make them less slippery. Grinding a cube into dust with the box of her pointe shoe, she looked down and over her shoulder in Madame Rousseau's direction. "Well, it's been more nothing-than-all lately. That still doesn't mean I should settle for the first handsome man who falls at my feet." She snorted and turned around, pointing at the spot where Law had fallen preceded by his dusty sneaker prints. "He actually tripped over his own two feet."

"Coordination was never Lawson's thing," Madame Rousseau admitted. She let out another dry cough, leaning on the doorway for support before looking back at Fanny. "But I've run the dance studio in this town for over thirty years. I know the people here like my own family and I guarantee that he's not the same feckless young man he was back then. You've changed since then, haven't you?"

"I have." Fanny stepped out of the box and walked to the doorway. "I've learned that the only person you can trust with your dreams is yourself."

"Is your dream still to perform?" Madame Rousseau asked gently. "You're still young, you know. Plenty of dancers come back from injuries."

Fanny rubbed her hip mournfully. "Not this one. I mean, I can still dance and take classes. But with the hip surgery, the doctor told me I can't lift my leg above forty-five degrees or I'll risk having to have a full replacement. The surgery was terrible. I'm not doing anything that might put me through that again. Plus, what show could I get where I can't kick higher than my knee?" She swallowed hard. Saying it out loud made it more real and more terrifying. "I'm going to have to find a new dream now. But don't worry," she said, forcing a smile. "While I'm here helping you, I'm taking the time to figure out exactly what my next passion is going to be. It's especially helpful that you're letting me live in the apartment over the studio for the next two months. Since I'm not performing, my equity insurance lapsed and I'm still on a payment plan from the hospital. If I don't find a way to make some more money soon, my new dream might be interior design for the cardboard box I'm living in."

"If it makes you feel any better, those little girls behind you all dream of growing up to be just like you." Madame Rousseau nodded at the barre. "Maybe one of them will follow in your footsteps."

As Fanny moved to the stereo to start the music for the warm-up, the weight of time sank heavily over her like a curtain dropping to the stage floor. She had been just like these little girls once, wistfully looking ahead to a life full of excitement and travel. Applause and rose petals. Waking up every day with a sense of purpose and passion. But she had learned since then that passion didn't just fall from the sky. There was no such thing as destiny. You chose your dream and then you ran as hard as you could toward it. That was how she had gotten as far as she had. Now she was starting all over again with no idea which direction she was running in.

The only thing she knew for certain was that she needed to run as far away as possible from men with great hair who were only interested in her until something distracted them and she was left crashing to the ground.

CHAPTER THREE

Usually, on the drive to the Longs' dairy farm for Sunday dinner, Law's mind was solely preoccupied with looking forward to the food.

The Longs and Carls had been getting together for dinner at least once a month as long as he could remember. His mom and Mrs. Long were sisters and while the food had always been good, it had become spectacular ever since BeeBee Long, his cousin who now ran the dairy farm, had married Bill Danzig, a professional chef who had worked on charter yachts and cruise ships. Now Bill operated a small dinner cruise boat that toured around the multiple lakes in the Mohawk Valley with occasional charters out in the Finger Lakes as well. The Sunday get-togethers typically featured dairy products from the Carls' dairy store that Law's brother Lucas ran with devotion to quality bordering on obsession, so every meal was like dining at a five-star restaurant in Europe minus the dress code and snooty waiters.

This time, however, he couldn't get his mind off the woman back at the dance studio. Why had she seemed to dislike him so much? It was both unusual and perplexing. He had tried to break the tension with a few jokes, but that had only resulted in him losing his shoes and a tiny bit of his manhood with the tutu that was too tight for anyone over the age of eleven. For crying out loud, the whole reason he had been there was to help. That was pretty much his whole reason for being anywhere in town lately. Not that he minded. It kept him occupied and people paid generously enough for his various services that he could afford his admittedly minimal expenses. But sometimes being Handyman Law got a little tiresome, especially when all he got for his troubles was a sore toe and pesky dreams about a beautiful stranger who despised him for no reason.

It was driving him crazy. Instead of thinking about the delicious meal he was about to devour, he was trying to figure out what Fanny's real name could be. Francesca? Frances? She didn't look like a Frances, but then again, who did except for grandmothers with glasses and lace-collared blouses? She was clearly an incredible dancer—that much was obvious even to a klutz like him. Would she be staying in Crystal Hill or was this just a temporary break in her performing career? Most vexing of all was the strange feeling that he had met her before. Was it possible he had met her on one of his travels over the years? He had met a lot of women and enjoyed their company for the short time he was in town, whether that town was Vail or Vancouver, and then he would be off to wherever the wind took him. He had always tried to be clear with the women about his intentions, something he'd learned the hard way after double-booking more than a few dates in his youth here in Crystal Hill.

Small towns were not the place to play the field, as the field was more like a small patch of grass.

That must be it, Law decided for himself as he pulled his Jeep up in front of the farmhouse and put it in Park. They must have run into each other somewhere exotic where she was performing and he had somehow not remembered her—there was that one time at the gong ringers' convention where he had playfully banged the gong with his head and ended up with double vision for a week. The good thing about this small town was that it was awfully hard to avoid people, and being the town handyman he spend his days running all over the place. At some point they were bound to see each other outside of the dance studio and he could explain everything.

Thoroughly satisfied with the mental resolution, Law slammed the door to the Jeep with such enthusiasm that it startled the water buffaloes who had been placidly munching at the metal wheel full of hay in the center of the pen.

"Apologies, ladies—er, gentlemen?" They all had horns, so it was hard to tell. He bowed at them jauntily, then swung his arms as he walked up the driveway to the white farmhouse. Tiny green buds were just starting to pop on the shrubs next to the steps. Spring in Upstate New York took its sweet time, but when it finally arrived, it was glorious. The field on his property would become a riotous palette of colorful wildflowers and sweet grass blowing fragrance into the breeze. He wasn't even close to being able to afford to build yet, so it would be at least another year before he could sit on his own front porch and enjoy it, though. Law knocked on the door and looked wistfully at the pair of rocking chairs to his left.

Suddenly the door swung open. His cousins, BeeBee and Jackie, the oldest sister out of the four Long girls, appeared with wide smiles.

The other two girls, twins Lindsay and Katelyn, were away at college.

"You made it," BeeBee exclaimed. She turned her head to the kitchen behind her, then looked back at Law. "Lucas and Chrysta are already here. They're getting Bell set up in her high chair."

"Something smells good," Law said as he wiped his feet on the mat before stepping inside. "What's Chef Bill cooking tonight?"

BeeBee shrugged. "Not sure." Crossing the room, she leaned on the counter separating the kitchen from the wide living room and called over the sounds of a spoon clanging against the side of a pot. "What's on the menu, Cappy?"

"Seared flat-iron steak with a spicy chimichurri sauce and spring vegetable ratatouille," Bill replied. He poked his head under the cabinets to drop a kiss on BeeBee's nose. "Fresh rolls are in the oven and dessert's in the freezer. Georgia dropped off a limoncello tiramisu earlier since she and Malcolm were taking Caroline shopping for an Easter dress."

Jackie sighed. "This time of year is so busy for everyone," she said, then added, tossing a rueful glance over her shoulder at Law, "That is for everyone who's married or has children. I'm glad you're here, Law. I was beginning to feel like the only single person on the planet here."

"I'm still surprised you didn't end up marrying some member of the royal family while you were living in England," Law teased his cousin. "Are you thinking about moving back there or are you staying here for good?" She had returned to the States for BeeBee's wedding last fall and everyone had expected her to make a quick return to the land of her authorial heroine, Jane Austen.

"I'm not going back to England." Jackie shook her head sadly. "It was…different than I thought it was going to be. A lot of things are, but being back here and seeing everyone starting their families made me realize how much I missed Crystal Hill."

"I get that," Law said. He lifted a hand to wave at Lucas, who paused an intense round of peekaboo to wave back. "Being an uncle is definitely the coolest job I've ever had and I've had a lot of jobs."

"Lucas was telling us how amazing you've been with Bell," Jackie said as they followed the tantalizing smell of herbs and sizzling steak into the kitchen. "Doesn't it make you want to settle down and have babies of your own?"

The question caught Law so off-guard he

walked right into the corner of the counter, jabbing his hip that was still sore from his fall at the dance studio last week. "Pump the brakes there, Jacks. I'm living in a tiny trailer that's full of sharp power tools and I'm too busy fixing broken water heaters and installing dry wall to even go on a date." He inclined his head toward BeeBee and Bill, who were setting steaming platters of food on the table. "Why don't you ask those two? The whole town's betting on when they'll pop out their first kid. We've got a running pool going at Big Joe's Diner."

BeeBee looked at Bill and grimaced. "Now I don't know if we can tell them. I don't want to get in trouble for insider trading."

Jackie clasped her hand to her mouth and rushed to envelop BeeBee in a tight hug, then pulled away to look at her belly, which was hidden, as usual, in denim overalls. "How far along are you?"

"Two months," Bill said. He wrapped his arm around BeeBee's shoulders and gazed at her with a look of such adoration it gave the whole room a warm glow. "We weren't going to make it town knowledge for another month, just in case. I told BeeBee we wanted to let you all know."

Lucas clapped him on the shoulder. "Congratulations, guys," he said, beaming down at BeeBee. "You're going to make such great parents. Plus, Bell can grow up with her cousin just like we grew up together."

Even though they all gathered around the table and sat together, Law suddenly felt as isolated as if he were back on his land, moving pavers around just to feel like he was making progress on something in his life. He had only been half joking about his living situation; he was by no means ready for a wife or kid. But the last decade of rootless wandering had left him playing catch-up to his younger brother and now his much younger cousins. It made him anxious, an emotion he didn't have a lot of experience handling.

BeeBee saying his name drew Law's attention away from his pity party and back to the real-life celebration.

"Sorry, I zoned out for a minute there," Law apologized, using tongs to grab a few slices of steak from the platter and putting them on his plate before looking across the table at her. "What did you say, BeeBee?"

"Just that Bill and I were hoping that you would design the baby's nursery for us like you did Baby Bell's," BeeBee said, clasping hands with Bill as she looked across the table at him.

"Erm…" Law unconsciously flexed his right hand under the table as if remembering its former glory. With his brother's help, he had turned his dad's former office into the most beautiful nursery, with a hand-painted mural of Crystal Hill, crown molding designed to look like scalloped clouds above the sky blue walls, and a crib Law had carved himself with such intricate designs on the corners it wouldn't have been out of place in a royal nursery. This had been before the accident. Now he wasn't sure it would be possible for him to do that kind of detailed work. Even if he could, it would take forever. BeeBee's kid would be walking before the room was finished. "You know what? I'll call in a favor with my buddy Sarge and ask him if he'll do it. He runs the comic book store in Bingleyton, but he's an amazing artist. Went to some big design school in Manhattan and everything. He'll do a much better job than I would."

"So, what are you saying? That my baby got the cut-rate nursery?" Lucas said indignantly. He reached across the table and pulled the platter of bruschetta away from Law just as he was reaching for it. "No mozzarella for you. I'm revoking your free cheese privileges."

Law glared at his brother and stretched his right hand out meaningfully. Lucas was the only one who knew that Law hadn't fully recovered use of his hand, and the only reason even he knew was because he had asked Law to help him sort the curds from the whey at the cheese shop and Law had only been able to work the spinel for a few minutes before having to take a break.

Lucas's gaze followed the movement and he grimaced. "Sorry," he muttered, shoving the platter back toward him. "Here. Take the big one."

The pity was even worse than missing out on free cheese.

"As long as your friend doesn't paint superheroes on my baby's wall, that sounds great," BeeBee continued.

"Ugh. I've never been a big fan of the superhero genre," Jackie said, then her eyes brightened. "Now, if they made a comic book with Mr. Darcy as the superhero, that would be a different story. Except it would have to be the same story, because you don't mess with the perfection that is Jane Austen."

"I don't know," BeeBee said with a wicked smile. "I think Jane Amarillo could do with a little reboot action. Instead of walking around gardens or writing letters, Mr. Darcy saving the world from mutant aliens would be a nice change of pace."

Jackie gasped and clutched her chest as the rest of them roared with laughter. "Mr. Darcy would never," she said when she had recovered the ability to speak.

"Would never what?" BeeBee continued to poke. "Save the world or wear one of those unitards all the comic book heroes wear?"

"Now, that's something you'd never catch me in," Law said, stabbing the bruschetta with a fork and plopping it onto his plate. "Maybe it's just me, but I kind of think if you're walking around in tights, you're not going to scare off many bad guys. I mean, it's not exactly the most intimidating look. In fact, I can't think of anything that would make me feel more vulnerable."

BeeBee snorted. "The idea of you being vulnerable is even more laughable than a Jane Austen comic book, Law. Nothing gets to you. You just keep bopping along with a smile on your face no matter what happens. No wonder everyone likes you. You're like the definition of easygoing."

"Yup, that's me," Law said, trying to ignore the tingling in his index finger. He had been so distracted by the disconcerting concept of wearing tights around town that he had gripped the fork the way he used to before the accident. It was so frustrating that he could carry heavy loads no problem, use a chainsaw without issue, but certain small motions, like twisting his wrist and pinching his fingers together, made his entire hand go either numb or feel like it was on fire. But if he told anyone that, they would stop hiring him or even worse, look at him with the same pity Lucas had. "Easygoing Handyman Law."

"So, what does a handyman do exactly?" Jackie asked, delicately spearing a grape tomato and popping it in her mouth.

"Well, generally, anything anyone needs," he said. "But I've been mostly doing outdoor home maintenance, minor wiring and home repairs. I was helping out at the dance studio last week."

BeeBee shook her head. "Poor Madame Rousseau," she said sadly. "I heard her coughing all the way across the street when I was delivering the milk to Lucas last week. She's in really rough shape."

"Running the dance studio is a lot of work," Jackie said. "Remember how long Lindsay would be there during rehearsals for the spring recital? Hours and hours. I can't imagine anyone else doing it, though. Madame Rousseau knows that place inside and out. They've even used the same sets and costumes for years."

"Hmm." Law lifted his eyebrows as inspiration hit. If he volunteered to build sets for the recital, he would be spending a lot of time with the mystery dance teacher. He'd seen the sets—they were simple enough builds and he could get some friends to do the painting and the finer details his hand wouldn't allow.

"You know," Chrysta added, raising her glass to Law. "What you do sounds an awful lot like a general contractor. If you got a license, you'd be able to take on bigger jobs and make more money. As a contractor, you'd also be able to hire a crew so you could delegate the, um, smaller tasks."

The way her eyes flicked briefly down to his hand made him suspect that Lucas had told her about his pain. That wasn't surprising. They were literally the perfect couple, finishing each other's sentences, sometimes not even having to talk out loud, instead just bursting into random fits of laughter at some inside joke. Not that Law wanted that kind of monotony. This fun uncle still wasn't ready for the promotion to husband and dad. But the idea of moving up in his career was appealing. Plus, at some point he was going to have to actually move beyond switching pavers from place to place and actually start building his house. That would require a lot more money than his handyman jobs brought in.

As usual, the Universe was telling him what to do next. Well, the Universe by way of his brother and sister-in-law. It didn't really matter where the direction was coming from, though. Whoever it was obviously knew what they were doing, so all he had to do was follow the signs wherever they led. An easy path for easygoing Law. That was all he wanted—that, and the name of a certain green-eyed dance teacher. Fortunately, the Universe—aka his cousins—had blown him toward the idea of building the sets for the dance studio, so that was on its way to being sorted, too.

Really, anyone who said life was hard just needed to relax and eat some cheese with a few friends and all their problems would be solved.

"So, if you're helping out at the dance studio, does that mean you saw the dancer who's helping Madame Rousseau out for the recital?" Jackie asked Law. There was a tentative note to her soft voice; then again, Jackie was as characteristically soft-spoken as BeeBee was blunt. Law was perpetually surprised tiny cartoon bluebirds weren't sitting on the woman's shoulders.

"I did," Law answered, eyeing the dessert on

the far end of the table. "Bill, do my eyes deceive me or is that tiramisu?"

"Lawson Carl," BeeBee thundered and everyone at the table jumped even though he was the only one in the path of the storm. "Please tell me you didn't brain dump what happened with that girl the last time she was in town as a guest star for *The Nutcracker*. I mean, I know ten years is a long time, but people in town still talk about that scene at the diner."

The scene at the diner. Ten years ago. Images clicked into place in Law's head like joists sliding into a beam. Now he knew why Fanny seemed so familiar and also why she seemed so hostile.

A little heads-up from the Universe about that would have been nice. Now the path ahead seemed a little less easy and a little more like an obstacle course. An obstacle course set on fire with random tigers that jumped out of the flames at you.

CHAPTER FOUR

IF YOU WORKED in show business long enough, it was inevitable you would at the very least encounter someone famous one day.

Even though Fanny's performing career had been cut painfully short, it had lasted enough time for that to occur and she was so glad that it had. The celebrity in question, a former teenage sitcom star who had done a stint on Broadway, was now one of Fanny's best friends. Aside from being a rising star whose last two films had been nominated for big awards, she was genuinely one of the sweetest people in the world. Collette Grundstrom was in Europe filming a period film, but never missed their weekly FaceTime date to catch up on each other's lives.

Not that there had been much going on in Fanny's.

Collette, on the other hand, had more than just a role to announce.

"I can't believe you're getting married!"

Fanny shook her head as she held the phone in front of her with one hand and a croissant from Georgia's Bakery in the other. "You and Keith haven't even been together for a year, and for at least a part of that time, one of you has been on a different continent."

Collette's fiancé, Keith Ludminsky, was a professional hockey player and as big a star in his field as Collette was in hers. They had met while Collette was filming a Hallmark Christmas movie in Canada last summer.

Collette's smile turned dreamy. "I know. But it's like that quote from the Jane Austen adaptation I'm filming. 'Seven years might not be enough time to know some people, but seven minutes is more than enough for others,' or something like that. Keith is perfect, well almost." She rolled her eyes exaggeratedly. "Even I can admit that his dancing is deeply terrible. I literally never thought humans could be that uncoordinated and the man is a professional athlete, but I was FaceTiming him yesterday and he actually fell out of a chair."

Fanny looked both ways before crossing Jane Street to get back to the dance studio. Not that traffic was ever an issue here. It was the main shopping area in town with only one traffic light and yet it was so quiet you could actually hear the birds chirping in the trees surrounding the lake. Being on tour for years meant mostly big cities like Chicago or Tokyo, where you could barely hear yourself think. A place this peaceful almost seemed unreal, like the set of an idyllic Rodgers and Hammerstein musical come to life. "I guess that's not a deal-breaker unless he's auditioning to be one of your backup dancers," she joked. Fanny stopped to take a bite out of her croissant and closed her eyes with delight. "Sorry. I was momentarily transported to pastry heaven. This lavender cream croissant is amazing. It's better than the ones I had when I toured in Paris." The last time she had been here had been brief—freelance guest spots didn't require much rehearsal time—and the encounter with Lawson Carl had admittedly left a bad taste in her mouth. Another bite of the lilac-hued cream in the center of her croissant, however, and it might be enough to erase that memory. The pastry was that good.

"It's a problem when you're trying to put together a first dance for your reception through video and the choreographer quits on you last minute." Collette's voice increased in pitch like a distress siren on a ship. "It's less than two months 'til the wedding and it's turned into this really high-profile event. The Prime Minister of Canada is invited. We can't just stand there and sway!"

Fanny paused in front of the dance studio and not just because she didn't have a free hand to open the door. There was an opportunity here and no sense in wasting time waiting to see if Collette came up with a better option. "I'll do it."

Relief washed over Collette's delicate features. "Fanny, that would be a lifesaver. But, uh, the thing is you'll need a partner. It's why I didn't ask you in the first place. I didn't want to put you in that position."

Collette had visited Fanny in the hospital immediately after her injury. She had seen the pain, the frustration, the bitterness of those early days and knew exactly who was responsible for it. But now the reality had sunk in. Finding a new calling in life, whether it was learning to become a yoga instructor at an ashram in India or studying pastry baking in Paris so that she could recreate these incredible croissants, was going to take money. Collette's wedding planner was the most elite event planner in Los Angeles. The pay would be good and she wouldn't have to go through a long-drawn-out process to get the job. By the time she finished choreographing Collette's wedding dance and helping

Madame Rousseau at the studio, she would be financially prepared to fully immerse herself in the second act of her life.

"It will be all right," she said. "This is different than performing with a partner." That was something she had resolved never to do again, no matter the circumstances. It hurt too much. "I know you and Keith. I can put together something that will make you both look amazing."

Collette nodded. "That sounds perfect. Here's what the wedding planner needs. Since Keith and I don't have a whole lot of time to rehearse together, we need video demonstrations of the steps, preferably one eight-count at a time. You'll need to talk us through each step slowly—as in explain it to us like we're in your baby ballerina class. The last choreographer nearly had an aneurysm trying to get Keith to do a basic box step."

"Well, your last choreographer wasn't me," Fanny said confidently. "What song are you dancing to?"

"'It Had to Be You,'" Collette replied, her eyes turning dreamy. "On our first date, a busker was singing it on the street corner and Keith turned to me and said, 'This is our song now.'"

"You guys are the sweetest," Fanny said, swallowing the last bit of her croissant and more than a tiny bit of longing with it. "I can't remember the last actual date I went on. Being on the road with national tours doesn't exactly mesh well with long-term relationships. The closest I got to dinner and a movie was grabbing smoothies in between matinee and evening performances and binging old episodes of *Gilmore Girls* on the male dance captain's laptop." She hadn't minded at the time. Career before love had worked just fine for her for the last ten years. The only problem was now that her career was over, she wasn't sure she even knew how to date in the real world. Heck, she didn't even know if she wanted to.

"Are there any cute guys in that town you're staying in?" Collette asked with a sly tease in her voice. "Maybe a flannel-wearing Christmas tree farmer or a romance writer who has been unlucky in love himself?"

Fanny laughed. "You've been on movie sets too long, my friend. I've got to go, but I'll let you know as soon as I find a willing victim—I mean, partner."

She hung up the call and opened the door to the studio and walked up the stairs. By the time she reached the top, her hip was screaming in protest. She stopped to lean against the wall with one hand, leaning into a deep stretch

to dash. Mrs. Van Ressler needs her glass baubles dusted and I'm the only one she trusts to do it right."

"I'm sorry, but if that's not a euphemism, I'm going to need more of an explanation."

He threw his head back and laughed. "You're funny. Definitely not a euphemism, although it's not the first inappropriate handyman joke I've gotten since I started this whole thing," he said, gesturing to the tool belt at his waist before looking back at her with that searching expression that made her heart do a strange little flop. "I really do want to hear what you have to say. Want to meet for lunch at noon?"

Fanny narrowed her eyes at the Big Joe's Diner sign a block ahead of them. "Is there somewhere we can go where we can talk without half the town assuming we're on a date? I'd rather not be run out of town by a horde of your enraged ex-girlfriends."

"Now 'horde' is definitely not a flattering collective noun," he teased. "I think they prefer the term 'Lawson's ladies.' Or 'Carl-ites,' for the true devotees." He scratched his chin. "I do know a place we can talk in private as long as you trust me enough to take you out in the woods in the middle of nowhere."

"I don't," she answered promptly and truthfully. "But I trust the Mace in my purse and emergency button on my phone, so it's all good."

He laughed again, his shoulders shaking. Brushing against her as he passed, he said quietly, "I think you might be the funniest woman I've ever met."

A warmth where he had touched her spread like a flower opening its petals. Fanny resisted the urge to touch her arm and keep it safe. "I'll meet you back here at twelve. This is not a date, just so we're clear," she added whipping her head around to frown at him.

"Crystal clear, Fatima," he said, squatting down to pick up the box, still chortling to himself.

She was already regretting this and they hadn't even started dancing yet.

CHAPTER FIVE

Law was no stranger to doing hard things, but by the time he had carefully dusted his seventeenth glass bird in Mrs. Van Ressler's menagerie of expensive vintage Murano collectibles, he began to question all the life choices that had led him to this point.

Sweat beaded on his forehead and threatened to drip into his eyes. That wasn't what you wanted when you were cleaning very fragile and very expensive items. Seeing was kind of part of the deal.

From the check-in counter of the bed-and-breakfast Mrs. Van Ressler ran, he could hear her talking softly on the phone in Italian to her long-distance boyfriend, Luigi Giordano. Their love story went as far back as some of the antique glass fruit he moved on to after the last bird. After having fallen in love in their youth in 1960s Venice, the pair had broken up and gone their separate ways, but never truly forgot about each other. At Bill and BeeBee's wedding, they had reunited when Luigi, an investor and financial mentor in Bill's dinner cruise business, had flown all the way out to Crystal Hill to attend. The town rumor mill whispered that although he had gone back to Italy, that was only to settle things with his large business before he moved to the States to be with Mrs. Van Ressler.

Law was happy for her, especially when he overheard her let out a soft giggle. Hearing the austere Mrs. Van Ressler giggle was akin to the Mona Lisa suddenly sticking out her tongue at you. But he wasn't happy when he glanced over his shoulder at the grandfather clock in the corner. It was almost twelve and he still had an entire glass mélange of apples, bananas and oranges to dust. If he rushed through the job, Mrs. Van Ressler would think he was a slacker, or even worse, he might actually break one of the pieces that, with his luck, was probably worth almost as much as his entire trailer. His whole handyman business—and if he was being honest, his whole identity—hinged on being likeable Law, the guy who didn't let anyone down.

Rotating his shoulder at an awkward angle to save his wrist from the twisting motion that would set off his injury, he swept the duster in the crevices between the objects and ignored the image in his head of Fanny waiting in front of the theater for him.

"Mrs. Van Ressler?" he called out. "I'm just about finished here. Do you want to come and take a look just to make sure you're satisfied?"

He heard her chair creak as she stood and then her slow footsteps sounded along the wooden corridor separating the rooms. Finally, she appeared in the doorway. Her face still glowed with girlish happiness even though she had worked to rearrange her features into their usual disapproving mask. Leaning on her cane, she peered along the shelf and gave a quick nod.

"That looks fine," she said. Pulling a handful of cash out of her blazer pocket, she handed it to him. "Thank you for coming over so quickly. The company I use for cleaning contracted out a new batch of young people and, frankly, I just don't trust them with my valuables yet. One of them was listening to some sort of loud rock music in what sounded like Swedish while he was cleaning the rooms, and the other had extremely sweaty palms." She made a tsking noise with her mouth. "As if I would trust my antique Venetian glass to someone with sweaty palms."

Law held up his hands. "Nice and dry," he said, hoping the light in the room was dim enough not to show the glistening on his forehead. "So, I've got to run. But if there's anything you need, just give me a call. And I'd love if you took a moment to put a review on my Handyman Law Facebook page."

"How does one leave a review on Facebook?" Mrs. Van Ressler asked. "Do I type the review and send a picture of it to you?"

"Next time I come over we'll add a social media tutorial to my services," he said. Tossing off a salute, he turned and sprinted out the door.

By the time he reached the theater it was only five minutes after twelve, but Fanny was already there, looking annoyed as she tapped on her watch.

"I know, I know." He jumped the curb and reached her, his breath coming in huffs. "It took longer at the inn than I had expected. So much glass." He winced as a side stitch jabbed him in the ribs. "I got here as fast as I could."

"I'd say better late than never, but I'm kind of a stickler for punctuality," she replied. "You learn after years of performing in Broadway ensembles that if you show up late for your call time, you inevitably get the dressing room spot with the sticky counter and the cursed mirror that ages you five years."

He started to laugh, then stopped. "Ow," he said, grabbing at his right rib cage. "That'll teach me to skip cardio for the last decade." Taking his car keys out of his pocket, he gestured to his Jeep parked in front of the theater. "Your chariot awaits, milady. I have the perfect spot for us where you can propose to me in private, but I warn you," Law said, "I expect to be swept off my feet, and if you don't get down on one knee, my answer will be a resounding, 'Meh.'"

She snorted. "Please. All I'd have to do is bat my eyelashes and you'd say yes if I gave you an onion ring. Also—" she leaned to one side to peer at his Jeep then straightened back up "—I'm not riding with you."

"What don't you trust, my vehicle or me?" he asked.

"Given the ratio of mud to flap on your tires and the fact that you almost made off with my best tiara, let's just say both." Her head bobbed in a single emphatic nod that hurt more than the side stitch. "But if you'd like to ride with me in my Civic, you can be the navigator."

Hmm. He did like the sound of that. It sounded important, essential. But he wasn't going to let her know that and give in so easily. "And what makes you think I trust you enough to let you drive me into the woods?"

She held up a small wicker basket. "I went to the market and Georgia's Bakery and packed us a picnic lunch." Walking backward, she clicked a key fob at a red Honda Civic parked right behind his Jeep. Its lights flickered and she dangled the basket up over her head beckoningly.

He dropped his chin to his chest. "Fine. Lead the way, Little Red Riding Hood."

She let out a small sniff that sounded dangerously close to a smothered giggle.

After sliding into the passenger seat of her car, Law turned her words over in his head and something occurred to him. "Wait a minute, you were on Broadway? I thought you were a ballet dancer."

"I was." She nodded as she turned the car on and checked her mirror. "I danced with the American Repertory Ballet until I was twenty-five. But careers in ballet are notoriously short. Most retire in their early thirties and I knew I wouldn't be ready to stop performing so young. So I decided to make the switch to being an ensemble dancer in musical theater. I'd studied in pretty much every form of dance since I was little, anyway, so making the switch wasn't as difficult as you might think."

"Turn right at the stop light before the lake," Law directed her. He glanced at her out of the corner of his eye. She wore her dark hair down today and it rippled over her shoulders in soft, shiny waves. Amazing that she was able to contain that beautiful mass into such a tight, smooth bun for dancing, although when it was up he could see the long, graceful line of her neck. He wasn't sure which he found more appealing and he cleared his throat to get his mind off the image. "So, being on Broadway, do you sing as well as you dance?"

The corner of her lips turned up in a small smile. "Not at first. I'd never sung outside of the shower before auditioning for chorus work. But I worked with a really great vocal coach to prepare. I mean, I'm never going to be a lead soprano at the Met or anything. All I needed was to get good enough so that the director wouldn't have to pull me aside and ask me to lip-synch."

"Wow." She was more impressive by the second. "I can't imagine just putting myself out there like that." Law didn't do anything unless he was certain he could do it well. Life was hard enough. Why go through all the effort if you weren't guaranteed success? He flexed his right hand as it rested on his leg.

She shrugged. "It's what I had to do to keep performing as a dancer and that was all I've wanted to do since I was five years old," she said. The sharp tones in her voice blurred and softened like an Impressionist painting. "My mom was a ballet dancer. She was a rising star with Boston Ballet but she retired when she got pregnant with me. Her last performance was in *A Midsummer Night's Dream.* There were pictures of her dancing in it on the mantel over our fireplace and I used to stare at them when I was little, mesmerized by the way she looked like an actual fairy queen flying in the air." Drawing a deep breath, Fanny refocused on the road. "Are we almost to the scene of the crime—I mean, the lunch spot yet? It looks like we're going into a forest out of Grimm's Fairy Tales."

"Hey, you invited me to lunch," Law countered. "And you're driving. If anyone gets to call stranger danger, it's me."

"Fair enough."

They drove in silence for another minute, then Law turned his head away from the window to look at her again. "When I was a kid, I wanted to be an astronaut. And a rock star. And a professional hockey player. And a rodeo cowboy for a minute, until my dad took me to an actual rodeo and I saw how big the bulls were. Turn left on the gravel driveway up ahead."

She nodded and slowed for the turn, slipping him a sideways glance. "What's your point, cowboy?"

As she parked the car in the paved area in front of his foundation, he turned his body to face her. "Just that most people give up on their childhood dreams. You chased after yours and I find that deeply attractive."

She rolled her eyes. "You just can't help yourself, can you?" Waving her hand back and forth between them, Fanny said, emphasizing each word, "We. Are. Not. Dating."

He climbed out of the car and leaned one arm on the sunroof. "And why is that exactly? I'm single—for real this time. With all my handyman jobs plus babysitting my little niece, I haven't really had much time for relationships."

She got out and faced him on the other side. "Even if I could believe that—which I won't until I'm in town for at least a few weeks without being accosted by one of your paramours—"

"Paramours?" He snickered.

"It's a choice and I stand by it." She raised her chin in the air. "But regardless of whether or not you're single, I'm only in town for a few months to help Madame Rousseau with the recital. She went all the way to Boston to coach me for my first ballet competition when I was fourteen and got me all the way to the Youth America Grand Prix two years later. I owe her so much. But after the recital is over—" she walked around the hood of the car, swinging the picnic basket in one arm "—I'm off to pursue my next great passion."

"Which is?" Law unlocked the swinging gate of the fence he'd built along the perimeter of his one-acre lot.

Her eyes darted to the ground, avoiding his. "I, uh, don't know yet."

"So how do you know you have to travel for it?" Law asked, pivoting and walking backward to try to get her attention. "What if your next passion in life is right here?" He gestured to his own chest and grinned, stopping a few feet ahead of her.

"Okay, I'm switching the word of the day from *paramour* to *relentless*," she said, jabbing a finger at him, but unable to keep the smile off her face. "You are relentless. I don't mean a passion for a person. I mean a passion that drives you, gives you purpose. It's what you wake up thinking about first thing in the morning, what every cell in your body longs for even when you're tired or sore. That was dance for me," she said with a wistful sigh before looking up at him resolutely. "But I, like most people, am multifaceted. I know I need to do something creative..." She hoisted the picnic basket on her elbow to tick a list off on her fingers. "Something physical. I don't want to be chained to a desk. I'm definitely an extrovert, so it has to be something where I get to interact with people on a daily basis. I have a Zoom call with a life coach scheduled for two weeks from now and I started making a list of these things so I'm prepared for the call."

"You gave yourself homework," Law said, blinking incredulously. "Fanika, you're a nerd."

"Getting colder with the names," she said. Twisting her body, she surveyed their surroundings. "Um, where are we?"

Law spread his arms out wide. "Welcome to my home." He stepped inside the gap in the front line of pavers and pretended to open a door. "Come inside. Please note the mat that says 'Lose the shoes, pants optional.'"

"Pants are definitely staying on," she said. "Are walls optional? I have a feeling this natural air-conditioning approach is going to lose its appeal in the winter."

"It's a work in progress," he said. "My parents gifted me the land. I actually live over there." He pointed to his trailer parked on the far end of the property along the tree line. "Right now I'm trying out a bunch of different layouts to see which one has the right feel to it. You can get these home design plans online that are really cool. The one I'm trying out now is a small log cabin."

"I see." She set the basket down in the center of the square of pavers. "Is this all right for dining or are we in the bathroom right now?"

"Laugh all you want, but it's going to be gorgeous," he said defensively.

She sat cross-legged on the grass, wrinkling her nose and putting a hand on her hip before stretching one leg out on the ground to the side. "I'm sorry. No sarcasm this time, either. I'm a huge believer in having a vision and I'm sure you'll be able to make yours come to life here."

He sat down across from her and opened the basket. A small blanket was folded on top and he flapped it in the air with dramatic effect before laying it on the ground. "I like the way you put it. Having a vision sounds much more grand than not being able to afford a sewer permit yet."

"But surely you have some idea for what you want your life to be?" She tipped her head to one side, then busied herself unpacking a small loaf of French bread and two containers of yogurt. "I mean, how else will you know what kind of house plan to build? If you want a family, you'll need at least three bedrooms. Or if you plan to work from home, you might need an office for your handyman empire." Taking out some grapes and a presliced salami, she finally handed him a bottle of soda. Orange, which happened to be his favorite.

"I mean, I know I'll need a guest bedroom for my parents to stay in when they come up to visit from South Carolina," he said, cracking open the bottle of soda and taking a long swig. "But as for the rest of it, I guess I'm just going to see where life takes me as I'm building. I can always build on an addition or second floor if I need more room."

She looked down at his hands. "Either you're incredibly full of unearned confidence or you're the handiest handyman in the world. That kind of work sounds like it would take a lot of skill." Fanny popped a grape off the bunch and tossed it effortlessly into her mouth. "What if you go through all the work of building this and life takes you somewhere else?"

"First of all, my confidence is earned," he said, gesturing with his thumb at his chest. "I used to be something of a woodworker before I injured my arm. I turned my dad's old office into a nursery and built my niece a hand-carved crib. Additions and second floors are more like putting giant Legos together. I can do that no problem. Second of all, I've done my share of wandering. Crystal Hill is my home now and I'm not going anywhere."

"I guess it's my turn to be impressed," she said. Opening up the container of yogurt, she took a plastic spoon out of the basket and scooped a mouthful before continuing. "I've been on the road touring first with the ballet company and then with various musicals and showcases for years, and I can't imagine putting down forever roots in one place yet. Not unless my calling is tied to one specific location, but I don't really see that happening. Ooh, I should add that to my list for the life coach," she said, raising her spoon in the air. "Location flexibility and traveling. I'd make a good flight attendant, don't you think?"

Law furrowed his eyebrows. One the one hand, she would look gorgeous in a flight attendant uniform. On the other hand, he didn't like the idea of her flying off to destinations unknown and never seeing him again. He drained the last of his soda and put the bottle back in the basket. Tearing the baguette in half, he handed one piece to her before taking the other for himself. "So you said you had something you wanted to talk to me about on this non-date?"

"Oh, that's right." She set the baguette down on the blanket and brushed crumbs off her hands, then folded them in her lap before looking at him with those piercing, green eyes. Law was quite sure he would say yes to anything she asked him right up until the next words out of her mouth. "I need a dance partner and I want it to be you."

CHAPTER SIX

FANNY WASN'T THE type to suffer from an excess of ego. Dancers, who spent most of their days in front of mirrors having their teachers point out every tiny flaw in a movement, were a uniquely self-critical breed.

However, she had at least expected Lawson to say yes to being her dance partner.

Instead, he recoiled as if she had told him the salami's expiration year had started with a one. "Fanny, I'm sorry. I—I can't do that."

She blinked. What was happening? Not only had he been flirting with her for the last several days, he was in her debt after the way he'd humiliated her ten years ago. Now she was asking him for the simple favor of dancing with her and he said no? Maybe he was confused. It was a lot to ask for someone that good-looking to also be quick on the draw. "Let me explain. Have you heard of Collette Grundstrom?"

"The actress? Of course."

"Well, she's getting married in seven weeks," Fanny explained, her hands waving in front of her as she spoke. It was a nervous habit, but his refusal had her rattled. "The wedding's in LA and it's going to be this huge affair with celebrities and *People* magazine profiling it. The problem is her fiancé is a professional hockey player with two left feet."

The clouds darkening Law's face cleared and his eyes brightened with recognition. "Oh, yeah. Keith Ludminsky. He's one of my favorite NHL players. I used to play hockey in high school," he added, his chest puffing slightly.

"And that's another reason why you're the perfect partner," Fanny exclaimed. "Collette wants me to choreograph their first dance, but Keith is hopelessly uncoordinated and they're both frequently out of town for their jobs. I'm going to record videos of the dance a few steps at a time. That way Keith and Collette can watch them and rehearse when they're able to get together. We can do a few sessions over Zoom or FaceTime, too, but for all of it, I need a dance partner." She clasped her hands together to make them stop moving. "I need you. As a dance partner, that is."

"But..." Law bit his lower lip and leaned back on his hands, looking around him as if trying to find the right answer in the trees. "You've got to know plenty of professional guy dancers who would be better for this. Someone you worked with in a musical or a ballet dancer. Why not ask someone like that?"

"Because someone like that is out of my price range," she said, forcing the exasperation out of her voice. "I need the money her wedding planner will pay me to travel for my next calling in life, once I figure out what that is. I can't afford to split that fee with a professional dancer. Plus, since I can't work with Keith in person, it will help to have someone who is closer in ability to him as I'm choreographing the steps."

"So, your way of asking me to do a favor for you is saying that you expect me to do it for free and you're calling me uncoordinated in the process?" He lowered his chin and raised his eyebrows at her. "I hope you aren't looking at sales as your next calling in life."

"Har har." She rolled her eyes. "I had hoped you would be happy to prove that you are actually a nice guy and not the same unreliable man-child you were ten years ago—that's why I hadn't planned on offering you a portion of the commission. I'd be willing to negotiate some compensation for your time, although as the choreographer and the professional, my cut would reasonably be much larger."

Law's face changed from defiant to properly chastened, then scrunched into a conflicted mask. "I really do want to help you and not just to prove that I've changed." His blue eyes searched hers for a moment, then closed as he shook his head. "But I can't do this for you. I really am sorry."

Fanny's shoulders slumped in disappointment before she flipped her hair off her shoulders nonchalantly. "Oh, well. If you can't, you can't. No biggie."

Shifting his legs under him to a kneeling position, he reached forward and touched her lightly on the knee. "It's just that, well, I'm applying for my general contractor's license and on top of my handyman job, I just don't have time for anything else right now. You can understand that, right?"

"Oh, sure, sure." Fanny feigned agreement. Even though her stomach seethed at the unexpected rejection, her mind clicked into planning mode. A dancer never stopped just because she got one no. If that was the case, Broadway would cease to exist entirely. "I'll just have to hold auditions. There are plenty of dance dads who would be glad to help out. I've seen lots of guys around town who look like they're in decent enough shape to do the lifts."

He scoffed, but since he, unlike Fanny, was not a professional performer, it was blatantly insincere. "Oh, please. Like who?"

"I mean, they don't call Joe Kim's diner 'Big Joe's' for nothing." She sat back and enjoyed the way red splotches appeared on the side of his neck. "I can put up some flyers in Bingleyton, too. It's only a few minutes' drive. Probably lots of strapping young klutzes out there." Turning away so he couldn't see her smile, she started packing up the food and putting it back in the basket. "I'll put up some flyers at the studios for the students to pass around and advertise on the community Facebook page. I'm sure Madame Rousseau will let me hold the casting call at the dance studio. There aren't any classes on Fridays." She closed the lid on the basket and smiled benevolently at him. "So if you know anyone, pass the word around, okay?"

Crouching back on his heels, he gathered one end of the blanket as she gathered the other. They met in the middle, their knuckles grazing against each other. Despite the fact that it was a warm day and sweat darkened the neck of his shirt, the citrusy scent of his cologne smelled fresh and enticing. Fanny had to force herself not to lean in closer to his neck and bury herself in the fragrance.

"I really do wish I could help you," he said, his voice low and earnest. Releasing the blanket and settling it into her hands, he reached into his back pocket and pulled out a small white rectangle. "Here's my handyman card. If anything at the studio needs fixing, just give me a call or text."

"Well." Fanny held the blanket to her chest with one arm and took the card from him with the other hand. "It is a very old building."

After she drove him back into town and dropped him off at his car, she climbed the second flight of stairs next to the studio to the attic apartment Madame Rousseau had cleared out for her. It wasn't large, but there was a small porthole window overlooking Jane Street and an antique, wire-framed bed. A wooden bedside table painted with pink roses on the front drawers housed a glass lamp that looked like a tulip. Madame Rousseau rented this room to guest artists teaching and performing with the dance school as Fanny had several years ago. Fanny wouldn't be staying here long enough to necessitate any changes to make it her own space. Save one.

Hanging on the planked wall above the bedside table was a square wooden corkboard. This board traveled with Fanny wherever she went on tour, had hung in hotel rooms all over the world. When she had danced with the ballet company, it had been filled with pictures of the great classical roles she hoped to dance—Giselle, Aurora, Juliet—and choreographers she wanted to work with and bits of ribbon from the pointe shoes she had worn during her best performances. After her transition to dancing in musicals, the images changed to cities the national tours would travel to, like Paris, Stockholm, even Casablanca—the title city of her favorite movie—and printed lyrics of her favorite numbers from each show. The vision board both kept her present in her passion and gave her goals to work toward in the future.

Now it was empty. The vacant cork stared back at her, pleading for a new vision. A new passion to fill her days and her dreams. Fanny grabbed her dance bag out from under the bed and dug around until she found the magazine she had bought at a bodega in Queens where she had been staying with a friend from tour a few days before coming to Crystal Hill. On the cover was a picture of Collette and Keith with the headline, "Wedding of the Year." She carefully tore the cover off at the seam and pinned it on the board. It wasn't the same as her childhood dream of dancing *Sleeping Beauty* at Covent Garden or her adult goal of performing as Louise in *Carousel*—the former even Fanny admitted was a bit lofty, but the latter she had actually achieved. Yet it was something, and for now, something was enough to keep her going until the One Thing revealed itself.

Almost as an afterthought, she took Law's card out of her purse and stared at it thoughtfully.

Clearly, he still knew nothing about dance or dancers because if he did, he would have known they never gave up on something once they had their hearts set on it. A dancer's goal was to strive for perfection. In that pursuit, they heard their fair share of noes. That never stopped a real dancer and Law's no certainly wasn't going to stop Fanny from trying to get him to agree to be her partner for this project. It wasn't that his performance at her baby ballerinas class last week had given her the impression of any latent natural dancing ability or that she had succumbed to the charms he clearly used to skate through life. She needed him to be her partner because she knew exactly what to expect from him. He had fooled her once, but the old adage of "fool me twice, shame on me" wasn't going to apply, because unlike her previous partnership, there was zero chance of any kind of romantic attachment between them whatsoever. That was the last thing she needed.

Over the next three days, she passed out flyers to all the dads at the dance studio, posted on the community Facebook page and hung clipboards with sign-up sheets at the local businesses, including The Crystal Hill Dairy and Cheese Shop run by Law's brother, Lucas. She wasn't expecting a large turnout, but was pleasantly surprised on Friday when the corridor of the dance studio was lined with half a dozen men. Most of them were dads with their daughters and wives in tow, their cell phones ready like stage moms at a beauty pageant. However, Joe Kim was there, too, along with Marco, the son of the owner of Mama Renata's Italian Ristorante. Fanny smiled encouragingly at them as she opened the door to the studio and gestured for the men to come inside. Peering around the corner, she looked from side to side for a familiar, broad-shouldered shadow and felt her hopes slide. She had asked Madame Rousseau to have Law come and install new smoke detectors in the studio that morning, as jealousy alone was not enough to rely on. Maybe he was tied up at one of his other handyman jobs. Dejected, she started to close the door, then a low voice humming softly above a heavy tread on the steps caught her ears. Covering her smile with one hand, she pulled the door closed with the other, but only halfway.

Walking into the center of the room, she pivoted to face the six men lined up at the barre. Several of them were leaning against it as if it was the type of bar where a cold Bud Light could be slid down to them by a world-weary bartender. Fanny resisted the urge to scold. They didn't know how sacred the barre was to a dancer, how it was the place where your lifelong dream began, your home base no matter how far across the world you traveled. The barre was always the same.

Clearing her throat, Fanny spoke in a voice several decibels louder than she would normally use, her body angled slightly toward the door. "Good morning, gentlemen," she said. Tucking a tendril of hair that had come loose from her French twist behind her ear, she opened her hands and extended her palms out to the men. "I'm so pleased to see so many of you here today for the audition. Now, you should know, this is a very unique opportunity. You see, I'm not looking for someone with dance training or even a whole lot of coordination. The dance I'm choreographing is for a very special wedding, and as the bride and groom are celebrities—I can't say publicly who, but most of you probably know them—and they have to travel often for work, it will involve recording small sections of choreography at a time to send to them to practice on their own, and then weekly Zoom sessions when they're able to rehearse together. It's a tight timeline as the wedding is in six weeks, but I have a fair amount of flexibility in my schedule so we can work together to get this done in a timeframe that fits the demands of your busy lives. Sound good to everyone?"

From the mirror to her right, Fanny could see Law hanging around in the hallway just beyond the door, inspecting a screwdriver with far more intensity than one would imagine necessary. She bit her lip and clapped her hands.

"All right, fellas," she called out. "Let's get to work."

She demonstrated several simple steps for the men: a box step, a basic cha-cha and a three-step turn and had them practice them individually. Nodding encouragingly and adding instructions for the few who were struggling to master them, she kept one eye on the hovering reflection in the mirror who appeared to be muttering a running commentary to himself.

"Very good," she said. "Now to get a sense

of your natural musicality and rhythm, let's try these to music. Just so we're clear, this is not the song the bride and groom have chosen for their first dance."

Scrolling through the playlist on her phone that connected to the wireless speaker, she tapped on the one song that was guaranteed to get even the most uncoordinated man on the planet moving along, "Eye of the Tiger." Sure enough, as soon as the first four notes sounded, the work boots planted on the other side of the studio entrance started tapping. The six men inside the studio simultaneously lifted their chins, meerkat-style, and began involuntarily bobbing their heads as the beat picked up. Fanny took them through the steps for several repetitions before turning the music off.

Outside the studio, she heard Law groan, "Aww, just before the best part."

"Okay, we've got some real contenders," she said, pointing finger guns at the men with a wink. "See what I did there? So the next thing I'm going to have you do is come forward, one at a time, and do these same steps, but we're going to do them facing each other as a couple. Number one, would you come on up, please?"

Joe Kim plucked at the card with the number

one pinned to his shirt as he walked forward. "That's right, guys. I'm number one."

"Well you were the first one in line this morning, but I like the swagger," Fanny replied with a grin. "All right, face me and put your hands out like this." She held her arms out in front of her and took his hands in hers. "We're going to do the steps in order just like I showed you, but I'm going to mirror your movements, okay? The only difference is that instead of the three-step turn, I want you to let go of my left hand and hold my right hand over my head while I turn."

"What do I do while you turn?" Joe asked, his forehead wrinkling in confusion.

"Express yourself," she said. "This is your moment to freestyle and enjoy the music. Shake your hips, shimmy those shoulders. Just keep it all inside your dance space right there."

She hit Play on the music again and they started with the box step. It took two tries before Joe was able to remember to step back when she stepped forward and she was pretty sure he bruised two of her toes during the cha-cha. Gentleman number two, the dad of one of her tiny tots dancers, did a little better, but didn't blink the entire time, a terrifying smile frozen on his face as his wife held up her phone behind the door, laughing so loudly she could be heard over the music. The next guy completed the steps correctly, yet had Fanny regretting her encouragement of self-expression when he threw his left arm up overhead and would have broken her nose if she hadn't ducked in time. She could have sworn she heard Law gasp, as he had now dropped all pretense of work and leaned against the doorframe with his screwdriver clenched in his left hand.

The last one in line was Marco. He was a good-looking man in his later forties, with silver-streaked, dark hair and a strong profile. However, given that his pants were as form-fitting as most of Fanny's actual tights, she wondered how the man actually moved, let alone danced.

Taking her hands as she held them out, he pulled her much closer than the other men had. The smell of garlic and oregano hit her in a powerful cloud. They were fine smells if one was hungry and the aroma was rising off a loaf of Italian bread. As a cologne, they left her wishing the studio had a window she could open.

"Wow, that's, uh, quite a strong grip you have," she said as he performed a cha-cha with the most exaggerated hip rolls she had ever seen.

Before she could step back into her own dance space, he leaned forward and whispered in her ear. "It's working. He's so jealous he can't even see straight. Five more seconds and he'll be walking in here to punch me in the face."

Her chin jerked back in surprise. "How did you—?"

But before she could finish the sentence, there was a tap on her shoulder. Fanny whirled around and saw Law with a number haphazardly pinned to his T-shirt. "I moved some things around in my schedule. Is it too late for me to try out?"

Fanny whipped her head back over her shoulder and Marco winked before bowing slightly at the waist and stepping away.

"I don't know." She tapped her finger on her lips and pretended to hem and haw. "I mean, you'd have to learn the steps these guys have and you've been working on the smoke detectors all morning. I don't see how you could catch up."

His chin lifted indignantly. "Watch me." He started with the box step, somehow stomping on his own big toe in the process, but finishing it with only a small grimace. His cha-cha was completely devoid of any hip movement and his three-step turn wouldn't have passed a sobriety test, yet the fact that he was able to do them on the first try from watching across the room was a good sign. He finished the last step and grinned triumphantly. "See. Not bad, right?"

It was bad, actually. For a dancer, anyway, but that was precisely why she needed him. He and Keith were like uncoordinated twins separated at birth.

"So, you can do the steps," she said with a nod. "Now let's see if we can dance together." Holding out her hands, she lowered her chin and looked up at him. "Come on. I won't bite. Unlike my tiny tots ballerina class from yesterday."

"Sorry about that," the mom waiting in the hallway outside called out from behind her phone. "We're working on the biting."

"No worries!" Fanny waved a hand at her, then shifted her gaze back to Law, who looked suddenly uncertain of what to do with his hands. She took a step forward and gently took his hands in hers. "When I step forward, you step back. Mirror my movements, okay?"

"Okay." He took a deep breath and gave her a tentative smile. It was so sincere, so unsure and completely out of character from his usual bravado. What was it about this side of him that was so appealing?

She started slowly on the box step, with his eyes trained on her feet. "Look up," she directed him firmly but softly. "Follow my lead. I've got this." His steps were shuffling, awkward, but that could be fixed. He took direction well and that was half the battle of teaching right there. "Now for the cha-cha, I want you to try to feel the rhythm with your hips. Fluid and side to side instead of up and down."

He lifted his eyes to hers and hooked an eyebrow up. "Bold of you to assume I've got any rhythm."

"Everyone has rhythm," she said as they cha-cha'd to one side. "When you swing a hammer or move a saw, there's a sway to the momentum. If you think of every movement as circular, you'll find the shapes your body needs to make."

He frowned, but the tension in his body lessened with the second cha-cha and it was slightly less robotic than the first.

"Now the turn," she said. "Lift my hand up to your face with one hand and guide my waist with your other. I'll do the rest."

The turn was where the other men had seemed to stiffen up with hesitance. Yet with Law, it was the exact opposite. He stepped in toward her, pulling her closer as he lifted her hand, and the assurance with which he placed his hand on her waist made her feel supported in a way she hadn't felt in a very long time. That single touch echoed what she had just said to him. "Follow my lead. I've got this. I've got you." As she glided in the turn past him, their faces came within a breath apart and she got another whiff of that fresh scent he wore, lemons and something woody. It was like a breeze coming down the hillside off the Amalfi coast. The scent combined with the surprising gentleness with which he handled her threw Fanny off-guard and she had to catch her balance to keep from stumbling.

She shook her head, then turned back to face the line of men watching them. "Well, uh, that concludes the audition for today. I'd like to thank all of you for taking time out of your schedules to participate. Make sure that you put your contact information on the sign-up sheet outside the door and I'll be in touch with more details."

As the guys began to file out, Law leaned in closer to her and jabbed an elbow into Fanny's ribs. "But I got the part, right, Fannah Montana?"

Any trace of his earlier vulnerability was gone. He was once again all bravado and charm, slapping high fives with the rest of the guys on his way out. But the more time Fanny spent with him, the more she wondered how much of that bulletproof charisma was really just an act.

CHAPTER SEVEN

"You would think one of the perks of living in a small trailer," Law grumbled to himself as he rummaged through his closet, "would be that you could actually find your sneakers quickly."

He was supposed to meet Fanny at the dance studio for their first dance session in ten minutes and he could not show up in the thick work boots he wore almost every day. As practical as they were for his handyman jobs—he never knew what people might ask him to do and having injured his hand already, was loath to lose a foot as well—they were not suitable footwear for dancing.

Being late would not be a great start to their partnership. In fact, not being able to find his sneakers was a bad sign in general. Clearly the Universe was telling him not to do this, if it was this much effort just to get out the door to meet her.

And the hard part hadn't even started yet.

"Dancing," he said to himself once again, sitting back on his haunches and shaking his head. "Why did it have to be dancing?"

His entire life he had been told he was a "natural" at so many things. Sports, music, making friends. He'd been able to fix or build anything since he was four years old and used the frame of an old bicycle wheel to sharpen a stick into a pretend rapier. But dancing? It was the one thing he could never do. It always felt like there was a short in the wire connecting his brain to his feet. Even when he got the lead role in the high school production of *Guys and Dolls*, he was told to stand in the back during the group dance number. Everyone had thought him such a gentleman when he was elected prom king and he graciously stepped aside for the royal dance so that the queen could dance with her date. Whenever he tried to move to music, he looked like a marionette controlled by a puppet master having a grand mal seizure.

Sighing, he reached into his closet one more time and dug around with one arm. His fingers grazed a shoelace, but when he tried to pull on it, something blocked its path to freedom. Law used his other hand to pry the object out and when it came free, he stopped for a moment to stare at it. One of his favorite carvings, a handful of which he couldn't bear to sell even though he had needed the cash desperately to get him through the time before he started his handyman business. The carving was a delicate mother hummingbird, floating just above her tiny nest, The ridges on the nest and each delicate feather had been carved with precision he could only dream of achieving now.

Tucking the small carving into the front pouch of his hoodie, he grasped his sneakers in his right hand and pulled them out of the closet. No excuses now, he thought as he wrenched the tongue of the sneaker open and shoved his foot into it.

It was a good thing he changed shoes, because he spent the entire drive into town kicking himself for changing his mind and agreeing to do this with her. Even though it was metaphorical kicking, it was still better to be doing it in sneakers than heavy work boots. Law just couldn't believe he had let stupid petty jealousy get the better of him like that. He had never been the jealous type before. On the rare occasion that a girl had preferred someone else to him, he hadn't let it get him down. Why chase after someone who wasn't into you? So even now, days later, he still found himself mystified by his own behavior. However, one thing that Law was big on was keeping his promises. When he said he would help someone, he meant it. As a handyman, as a friend, as a brother.

Speaking of which, Law's cell lit up with his brother's name just as he turned onto Jane Street. Law pulled into a spot in front of the dance studio and parked before answering.

"Hey, man," he said. "Funny that you called just now. I'm across the street from you. What are you, watching out from the window of the shop for cheese thieves and spies?"

"Okay, it can't be a coincidence that Gutfeld's Dairy just happened to put out a pepper Havarti two days before I released mine—you're making a joke, aren't you?" Lucas sighed loudly over the phone. "No, I'm calling because the lawyer who's advising Chrysta on franchising options for her business has an opening in his schedule this afternoon if you want to meet with him about setting up an LLC for your general contracting business."

Law wrinkled his nose. "But I don't even have my license yet."

"We were talking with him about it and he said that because the license will go through the local bureau and not the state, usually people set up their LLC before starting the license application," Lucas explained.

"I guess I have a lot to learn." Law puffed out his cheeks before exhaling. "This whole process is so complicated. It was so easy to start my handyman business. All I had to do was make up a couple of graphics online and post it on flyers and Facebook."

"I know the idea of running your own business is intimidating," Lucas said, reassuringly. "When Dad transferred the cheese shop to my name, it felt like I was being strangled in red tape and legal documents. But once you have your license, you can hire a crew for bigger jobs and make enough money to finish your house, maybe settle down and have a few kids." In the background, Baby Bell made a squawking noise loud enough for Law to hear. "Bell says she wants cousins before she's old enough to drive."

"Yeah, well, tell Bell if her daddy keeps nagging, Fun Uncle Law is going to buy her lots of noisy toys with flashing lights and spiky pieces perfect for stepping on with bare feet in the middle of the night," Law warned teasingly. "You know I need to take things one step at a time. With my coordination, I can barely even manage that much."

"I heard through the grapevine that the new dance teacher picked you to be her partner for the video she's making," Lucas said. "I guess you've tried every other job—might as well add backup dancer to your résumé. Do you get to wear a shiny costume?"

"The details of this project are top secret, Mr. Nosy," Law replied with a huffy sniff as he got out of the car and closed the door. Shielding his eyes with one hand, he stared pointedly across the street at the cheese shop. "Speaking of top secret, isn't that Gutfeld's sister walking down the street with a notepad in her purse?"

The curtain of the cheese shop ruffled suddenly with excitement. "Got to go," Lucas said, calling out before he hung up. "Chrysta, lock up my cheese lab. This is no longer a secure location."

Law snickered, then put his phone in the back pocket of his jeans before turning around to face the dance studio where a gorgeous woman was waiting for him to hold her in his arms. This was his chance for redemption, to show her that he wasn't the same flighty doofus he had been ten years ago, that he really could be trusted.

As long as he didn't accidentally break one of her toes or drop her, of course.

Taking the steps to the studio two by two, Law stopped and smoothed a hand over his hair before knocking on the door. When Fanny opened it, he gave her his best smile.

"Hello there, Fanneliese," he said, leaning his right hand on the doorway and propping his left on his hip, making sure to clench his biceps as much as possible. "Shall we dance?"

She arched an eyebrow at him wryly. "It's better than standing here listening to you guess my name wrong again."

"I will figure it out." He pointed a finger at her as she stepped to one side and gestured for him to enter the studio. As he walked, his sneakers made a squeaking noise on the clean studio floor.

"You can actually take your shoes off," Fanny said, taking in his shoes with a wrinkle of her long nose. "Today we're just going over some of the basic steps that we'll then build the routine off of."

"You're in luck," Law replied as he used one foot as a brace to slip the heel of the other sneaker off. "Building things happens to be my specialty." He slid the other shoe off, and holding the laces of both in one hand, tossed them over his shoulder like a scarf.

"That's actually a good analogy for what we're doing today," she said. "Think of this first session as the outline of your foundation. In dance choreography, we usually have a few base combinations that we'll then vary or layer on top of each other to create the finished dance."

Her encouraging smile sent his spirits soaring through the roof. Making other people happy was something that usually brought him an immense amount of satisfaction, but this was something new. Pleasing Fanny wasn't something that came as easily as setting up his old first-grade teacher's Wi-Fi, but the reward was ten thousand times greater and made him want to see what else he could do to make her smile.

"All right." He rubbed his hands together. "What's our first building block?"

She walked to the center of the studio, slowly and gracefully. Even her walk was like a dance. She faced him, and suddenly Law's bare feet made him painfully aware of the extra three-quarters of an inch he lost without his shoes. "Let's start with your stance," she said, squinting one green eye critically at him until it glinted like a cut emerald. "Have you always had a bit of a curve to your upper spine or is it more of a fatigue-induced slouch?"

"Slouch?" He lifted his chin and his shoulders at the same time. "I don't slouch."

"Don't get defensive." She held up both hands. "It's natural, especially for someone who bends over in his work a lot, to develop a hunch. It's easy to correct with training and, if necessary, a girdle."

Law took a step back. "I'm not wearing a girdle." This was not starting out the way he had thought it would. For starters, the word *girdle* was not one he had bandied about in his fantasies. "It literally has the word 'girl' in it."

She rolled her eyes. "Men," she muttered under her breath. "Fine. Roll your shoulders back and lift your chest. I tell my baby ballerinas to pretend they have a jeweled necklace on that they want to show off. So, um—" she tapped her lips with one finger "—pretend you have an Olympic medal for…handymanning and you want everyone to see it."

He stuck out his chest. "Like this?"

"Better," she said cautiously. "But don't let your shoulders come up." She pressed gently down on each shoulder with one hand. "Now keep your core nice and tight while your chin stays parallel to the floor."

It was so many directions all at once and they hadn't even moved yet. Law slid his eyes to one side to check his posture in the mirror and noticed that his face was turning bright red.

Fanny followed his gaze and her eyes widened. "Law, you also have to breathe."

He let out his breath in a huff and watched

his Superman posture disintegrate. "Why is this so hard?"

She smiled at him. "Dance is an intense form of athletics," she said. "It requires muscle control, strength and flexibility. It's why we start training so young. The posture takes years to become ingrained in your body."

Desperation and panic fought each other, producing a cold sweat on the back of his neck. "But we only have six weeks." This was why he didn't take on things he wasn't sure he could succeed at accomplishing. It was too much. "Are you sure we can do this?"

She shrugged. "Only one way to find out." Turning to face him again, she put her hands on his shoulders once more. They were only inches apart, close enough for him to see the small mole behind her right ear, the beginnings of smile lines next to her eyes. "Focus on your posture again. Shoulders back, arms relaxed, core tight. Try to think of your rib cage moving laterally as you breathe. Now put your hands on my waist."

So much for his breathing. He encircled her waist with one hand on each side just above the small curves of her hips. She was thin, but wiry and muscular. The whole dancer athlete thing wasn't just lip service. Law was pretty sure she could throw him over her shoulder if the choreography called for it. Impressive as it was, just the warmth of her skin was making him feel even more vulnerable than when she had suggested wearing a girdle. "Um, okay. Lateral breathing."

"Good," she said. "Do you remember the box step I taught at the audition?"

"Erm." Law really wanted to scratch his head to jog his memory, but that would involve his hands leaving her waist and that seemed like an impossible task at the moment. "Was that the hip shaking one?"

She let out a beleaguered sigh. "No. The box step was the one where your steps make the shape of a box. Follow my lead, okay?"

Law wanted to nod, but he was supposed to keep his chin up, so he simply said, "Okay." It occurred to him two seconds after she started to move that following her lead was going to be difficult when he couldn't look down to see her feet. Glancing quickly down, he saw that her right foot had moved backward, so he did the same. His hands were still on her waist, but now they were stretched apart like the one time he and Lucas had gone fishing and the boat had started to drift away from the dock. Law had clung to it for dear life, pulling it back to shore only to slip and fall into the water doing a celebration dance after catching his first fish. Just another example of how dance ruined all the good things.

"Law, you're not following me," Fanny said. Her voice grew a little sharper and it stung his already vulnerable ego.

Law finally let go of her and threw his hands in the air. "Do they really need to do a first dance?" he asked in exasperation. "What about a Just Married hacky-sack toss? Or a newlywed handshake?"

"Why are you giving up so easily?" Fanny frowned and grabbed his hands, placing them back into their former position. "Try again. This time, when I go backward, you go forward. A dance partnership is about balance, give-and-take, trusting that the person you're with knows what they're doing."

Had Law ever experienced that in a relationship? For all the women he'd dated—and there had been a number of them—he couldn't remember ever feeling that way with any of them. Maybe he had never allowed himself to feel that way. Because then he might have felt as useless and ineffective as he did now when they realized he wasn't perfect after all.

She slid her foot backward again and he

"Look at her face," Fanny replied, making a sweeping gesture with her hand over her own exquisite features. "Look at her smile. She loves it. That's what makes the difference. You can train someone to improve their posture and turnout, but if they don't love it, they won't do the work. If they're passionate enough, the sore muscles and bleeding toes and hours of rehearsal won't feel like a sacrifice. It's the one who loves it the most. And that's true with anything worth doing. You have to start with passion or there will always be a reason to quit."

A poster on the wall at the end of the hallway caught his eye. He jutted his chin at it. "Is that how you got there?" Walking past her, he moved toward the image of Fanny being lifted by some guy as her sparkling white dress billowed around her leg that stretched impossibly high behind her head. The photo was so enchanting that Law had to tear his eyes away from it to look back at the real-life Fanny standing motionless behind him. "Did you love it more than everyone else?"

"More than everyone and more than anything," she said softly. A sheen of emotion swept over her eyes, but before Law could reach forward to comfort her, she blinked and it was gone. "I mean, that is simplifying it a little bit.

I had incredibly supportive parents, including parents who were both dancers at some point, with the financial privilege to afford lessons and private coaching from Madame Rousseau for competitions that got me noticed by companies. But yeah—" her lips quirked up in a dimmed version of the thousand-watt smile she flashed in the poster as she turned and looked from it back to Law "—it was my passion that led me there."

One of the few things Law knew about dance was that in a partnership, the guy was supposed to do the leading. But he was beginning to suspect that he would follow this enigmatically fascinating woman anywhere she wanted to take him.

CHAPTER EIGHT

EVEN THOUGH THE poster was one of the most flattering photos that had been taken of her, Fanny hated that this was the one Madame Rousseau used to show off her former student.

Mainly because half of the photo was *him*. The self-centered narcissist whose vanity had robbed her of years of performing and touring. It was a shame, too, because as dance partners they had been perfect together. Perfect height difference for lifts, electric chemistry. They had moved together as if they were one person and for just a moment, she had taken her eye off the ball and conflated her passion for dance with a passion for him. It had seemed like a mutual passion whenever he brought her coffee to her dressing room and saved her a spot next to him at warm-ups. But she'd learned the hard way that other people never prioritized your dreams over their own. They always put themselves first, and Jason had made that clear when he moved on with the tour without so much as sending a card to her in the hospital.

As if reading her mind, Law tapped the poster over Jason's face. "Who was this guy?"

She inhaled sharply before answering. "He was my partner on the last two national tours I did," she answered, trying to keep her voice even. "We did *Chicago* together and when the same choreographer was hired for *Carousel*, he told the casting director about us and we were brought in for a special call. That almost never happens," she added, taking a few steps to stand next to Law. "But *Carousel* is one of those musicals with a 'dream ballet' sequence, so the choreographer was given a heavier hand in terms of casting. I heard through the grapevine that he's starting work on the tour for *An American in Paris* now."

There was no amount of willpower, even for a dancer, that could keep the bitterness out of her voice for that one. It was the dream job, the role played by Leslie Caron in the film, the one that required a triple threat who could do ballet at an elite level in addition to dramatic acting and singing.

Law wrinkled his nose. "He looks like a jerk."

Fanny's head snapped back. "What makes you say that?"

"For starters, he's holding the most beautiful woman in the world up in the air and he's not even looking at her," Law said. "His head is toward you, but his eyes are looking past you."

There was probably a mirror behind her, Fanny thought sarcastically. Yet the dancer in her felt obliged to defend one of her own. "The photographer might have told him to do that. This was for a promotional shot, not during a performance. It's different when you're just trying to take a good picture."

Law studied the poster again, then shrugged. "I stand by my statement. He should have been supporting you with everything he had, including his eyeballs."

Fanny blinked, knocked off-balance by the accuracy of his statement. There was no way he should have been able to pick up on something so subtle, especially as a nondancer. She could have kissed him for being so intuitive, and then he added, "I think it's his face. He's got one of those faces that's just asking to be punched."

Never mind.

"Since we're rehearsing a wedding dance, not the fight scene from *West Side Story*, how about we leave the punching out of the choreography?" Fanny suggested, taking him by the shoulder and guiding him back toward the studio where they had started.

"When do we start with the actual steps—the choreography?" He corrected himself and it was almost too adorable. Fanny reminded herself that Law's charm wasn't specifically directed at her. The man was inescapably likable. That wasn't reason enough to start thinking of him as anything other than a talking prop.

"Right now," Fanny answered, giving him a gentle shove through the doorway.

He turned and faced her with an alarmed expression. "Now? But what about earlier? You looked like you were ready to strangle me because I couldn't do a box step. I'm genuinely worried for my safety if we try actual dance steps."

"I wasn't frustrated because you made mistakes." Fanny put her hands on her hips. "You're a beginner, like the groom. I need to know what you can and can't do, so I know what he can and can't do. Mistakes are part of that. I was frustrated because you were giving up on yourself and masking it with your goofy shenanigans."

"Shenanigans?" He scoffed. "You've been in cheesy musicals too long, Fanibeth. No one uses words like that."

"Except for me because I just did." She smiled.

"Now let's stop all the palaver and get to cutting a rug."

His groan of pain was all the incentive she needed to keep talking like a character from an early talkie. The fact that they were dancing to a song written in 1924 didn't hurt either.

"So, there are two different versions of the song," she went on, switching back to her teacher voice. "The Sinatra version starts with a bridge lyric that most people don't know, but I think in the interest of time, we're going to go with the Harry Connick Jr. version that begins with the instrumentals before going right into the chorus."

"Hold up." Law put up both hands. "We're not going with Ol' Blue Eyes? I'm half-Italian. If I do this, my ancestors are going to put a blood curse on me."

She shrugged one shoulder. "Bride and groom's choice. Actually, wedding planner's choice. The guy planning their wedding is a big deal. At any rate, our job is to put together a dance that makes them look sensational and doesn't make them want to kill each other rehearsing it."

"Got it." He nodded.

She crossed the room and set up the wireless speaker in the corner, her filmy skirt swishing back and forth as she walked. Whatever her next passion turned out to be, Fanny hoped the uniform was equally as comfortable and beautiful as dancewear. After setting it up, she stood up straight and pointed at him. "All right, Law, you're center stage. Let's see your posture. If it helps, remember, Keith will be wearing a tux."

He immediately gained an inch of height by straightening his spine. Buttoning an imaginary vest, he gave her a hesitant smile. "Like this?"

"Much better." Using her phone, she started the song. Orchestral trumpets blared the symphonic introduction. Fanny winced and turned down the volume. "Sorry. So, you're going to stand there and reach your right arm out to your bride, aka me. Palm up. Now give me a kind of nod that says, 'Come here, you. Let's start the rest of our lives together.'"

He inclined his head away from her and even Fanny had to admit the man took direction well. She walked toward him as the music swelled and quieted, then took his right hand with her left. "Now spin me into you," she said loudly so he could hear her over the music.

He jerked his right arm and pulled her into him with such force that it threw Fanny off as she spun and she landed back against his chest with a thud. "Oof."

He cringed. "Sorry." Looking down at her, he

bent his head down until their foreheads were nearly touching to say into her ear. "I work in construction, so I'm not used to handling delicate cargo."

Fanny had worked with dozens of partners over the years, many of them very good-looking men. Something about the way Law held her felt different this time. More intimate. More real than it had been even with Jason. The memory of her former partner snapped her back to the task at hand. She needed this commission, so this time there was no room for distractions or feelings.

Breaking away, she hit Pause on the music. "It's, uh, fine," she said, fiddling with the bobby pins holding her French twist in place. "But the bride will be wearing a very large, full gown. Try to allow space for the dress as you bring me in. And a gentle pull is fine. Your partner is a lady, not an electric screwdriver. So reach out the hand, I walk—two, three, four—then pull—six, seven, eight."

This time he tugged on her hand gently enough to lead her without hurling her into him. With his right arm around her back, he waved his left hand. "Um, what do I do with this arm? It's just kind of hanging out over here."

"While I'm turning, keep that arm on your

imaginary tuxedo jacket," she explained. "Let's try that again with the music."

He posed with one hand extended to her, the other on his torso, and this time after she spun into him, she put her right hand on his chest. Under her palm, his heart rate suddenly tripled in speed.

"What are you doing?" he whispered, his blue eyes darkening with intensity.

"The choreography," she whispered back. Between the crooning vocals in the music and the way the clouds had moved over the sunlight streaming through the window, a spell seemed to have been cast over the room. Fanny realized her own rapid-fire heartbeat matched his as she slid her left arm behind his back. "Now put your left hand over mine, here." She patted his chest and he covered her hand with his like a warm mitten. "And draw my arm out to the side to make our dance frame."

He curled his fingers around hers and looked at their entwined hands as he pulled her arm slowly out to the side. "Like this?"

The next step was the box step, but as much as she commanded her legs to move, they wouldn't budge. It was as if they had created a bubble between them, a space that was safe and warm, where if she moved half an inch closer, her head could rest on his shoulder. Now she knew why some couples chose to simply stand there and sway. It wouldn't matter how many people were in attendance. If she and Law were the real bride and groom, they could stay just like this and it would be as if they were the only two people in the world.

But they weren't the bride and groom, Fanny reminded herself. They weren't a couple and she wasn't going to be ready to let any man in her life until she knew what that life was going to revolve around because she was for sure not going to let her passion rest in the hands of a man ever again. She was the captain of her own ship and her passion was her compass. It was the only thing that could keep her true, rather than accidentally guiding her into a storm.

Letting go of his hand, Fanny stepped back two paces and looked at her phone, hitting Pause on the music again. "You know what? I think that's good enough for today."

"Really?" Law actually looked disappointed. "But we only did the introduction. Don't we need to do more before we record the first video for the couple?"

Fanny continued to back away toward the door as she talked, still looking down at her phone. "We'll get to it next session. Do you have time to meet me tomorrow? That will give us another day to practice before we record on Friday."

"Um," he scratched his head and looked out the window over the barre that faced the street. "I, uh, guess so. I've got a couple of handyman gigs booked for the morning, but after that, I can stop by."

"Good," Fanny replied. "Good. I'll see you tomorrow around the same time, then." She motioned for him to exit. "Okay. Off you go. I've got lots of, uh, choreography stuff to take care of." Practically shooing him out of the studio, she closed the door behind him and put her hand on her heart. Yup, still racing. She went to the barre and stood on her toes, watching out the window to make sure he had left the building, then walked out into the hallway again. Propping her hands on her hips like Wonder Woman, she forced herself to stare at that poster again. Law might not have been the same kind of careless as Jason, but that didn't mean he wouldn't drop her heart the second she gave it to him. This was a gig, no different than any other she had been hired to perform. Each job was a stepping stone to the next and in this case, it was a bridge to a whole new adventure she simply hadn't chosen yet. The only way to make it across was to focus solely on getting the job done. She would see Law only for rehearsals and recording. The rest of the time while she was in Crystal Hill, she would be laser focused on the search for the next love of her life and that love was *not* going to be a man, no matter how expressive his blue eyes were when they focused in on her face.

The door to the other studio opened and the intermediate class filed out in a stream of sparkly leotards and high-pitched giggles.

Fanny checked the time on her phone. "Class is done already?"

Madame Rousseau ushered the last dancer out and sighed. "I let them out a few minutes early. The heat in this room isn't working and I don't want the girls to pull muscles doing their leaps in an ice box."

"I wish there was more I could do to help," Fanny said, crossing her arms over her chest and surveying the corridor. "You've put so much work into making the studio a successful business."

"It has been so much more than a business," Madame Rousseau said wistfully as she placed a wrinkled hand on the doorframe. "This town gave me a home, a family. Giving the young people a place to discover their love of dance was my way of saying thank-you. There's something special about this place, you'll see."

Fanny shifted her weight uncomfortably from one foot to the other. It had been a long time since she had felt "at home" any one place. Her family lived in New Jersey, but she had started intensive dance training in Manhattan at such a young age that she had spent more time on the train than she did at home. Even when she toured with the ballet company or a musical, the most she saw of any place was the theater, the hotel room or whatever local diner was still open after 11 p.m., when the show ended. The only constant of any location had been the dance studio, the mirrors, the feel of the barre, the lingering smell of hairspray and sawdust. She guessed she just wasn't the type of person to settle down in one place because of its charming scenery or colorful nightlife. Just like she had never been the sort to settle down with one person because of his roguish smile or the way it felt when he held her close. Following her passion had served Fanny well over the last several years, and that was how she would continue to do things.

"The town is lucky to have had a dance teacher like you over the years," was all Fanny said, though. She didn't really get it, but people around here had a strange connection to their town. The last thing she wanted to do was accidentally insult them by saying it was just another roadside stop to her.

"Why don't you pop out to the local pizza place, Mama Renata's, and get us some Italian sodas to go?" Madame Rousseau dug inside the cleavage of her leotard and pulled out a $10 bill. She coughed heavily once more, her hand trembling as she offered the money to Fanny.

"Of course," Fanny replied. "I can take the advanced pointe class this evening if you're not feeling up to it."

"That's so sweet of you," Madame Rousseau said as she held on to the wall and walked slowly toward the office door across the hall from the studio. "But I don't think it will be necessary. Those sodas do wonders for my energy."

Fanny threw on a denim jacket over her dance dress and slipped her feet into sandals. It was almost five o'clock, so there were actually a few cars out on the road as parents chauffeured their kids to evening activities and some of the businesses on Jane Street that opened early in the day like the bakery and the dry cleaner closed their doors for the evening. It was surprisingly warm for a spring evening in Upstate New York, with a light breeze that lifted the fragrance of the flowers bursting their colors out for display in the window boxes at the bed-and-breakfast. Okay, so the town's main drag was exceptionally pretty with its brick and slate stone buildings and colorful awnings waving a cheery hello from the doorways. But pretty wasn't enough for her to be sweet-talked into moving here.

Fanny needed inspiration.

She crossed the street, then stopped in front of the antique store. Pretending to admire a pearl ring in the window, she surreptitiously leaned backward and craned her head to peek into the shop next door. No sign of him in there, thank goodness. She half jogged past, ducking her head to one side and shielding her face with her hand, just in case. Mama Renata's was next to the cheese shop, a location that had to be by design. When she opened the door, Fanny stopped for a moment to inhale the smell of garlic in the air so thick she could almost chew on it. The lighting was dim and as she squinted to check the soda flavors written on the menu above the counter, a familiar set of broad shoulders came into view, and as the man turned, the light from the candles on the table highlighted the gold streaks in his chestnut-colored hair.

See, this was why she couldn't live in a town

like this. You were guaranteed to run into the one person you were actively trying to avoid.

She turned on her heel, preparing to flee and hope that an Orangina from the corner market two blocks down would suffice, when she nearly bumped into a tall brunette woman entering the store.

"I'm so sorry," Fanny apologized, feeling extra guilty when the woman grasped instinctively at her belly, which protruded ever so slightly above her mud-caked jeans. "I should have been more careful."

"Psshht." the woman waved her other hand. "If not-watching-where-I-was-walking was an Olympic sport, I'd have five thousand gold medals." Her eyes flickered over Fanny's diaphanous skirt attached to a leotard-style top. "Are you a new teacher at the dance studio? My sister used to take lessons there. She's in college at the University of Buffalo now, majoring in dance."

"Oh, no," Fanny sputtered, casting a quick glance back at the counter where Law was still obliviously drumming his fingers. "I mean, I am teaching there for now, but only until the spring recital is over. I'm only helping Madame Rousseau temporarily until she gets her strength back."

"That's nice of you," the woman said. She held out her hand. "I'm BeeBee Danzig. I run the Crystal Hill Dairy Farm. While you're here, feel free to stop by and visit the animals. My sister will be home for spring break in a few weeks and I'm sure she'd love to have someone else to talk about all things dance." BeeBee leaned forward and said in an exaggerated whisper, "I'd love it just so I don't have to be the one to listen to her."

"Thanks," Fanny said. "Um, I've got to get going, but it's nice to meet you."

"Fanny?" Lawson whipped around and threw his hands in the air. "What are you doing here?"

BeeBee waved a finger between them. "You two know each other?"

"Actually, I'm helping Fanny with a dance she's choreographing for a celebrity wedding," Law said, his chest puffing with pride. "I'm her partner."

"Ah, so that's why you don't have time to work on my baby's nursery." BeeBee whacked him playfully on the arm. "Hollywood calls and you don't have time for your cousin or her unborn child, so you farm out the job to some yahoo from Bingleyton."

So much for Madame Rousseau's theory of Law maturing and becoming more responsible. He thought he had a chance with Fanny, so he'd blown off his family and other obligations to chase after a girl he would probably get tired of after five minutes anyway. A tiger never changed his stripes. Well, seeing as how Fanny wasn't going to take any more of his time outside of the studio, he should certainly be free to help his cousin. "Oh, I'm sure Law can make the time to help you with your nursery. I mean, what kind of handyman would say no to a job like that?"

"It's not that simple." Law's face scrunched with frustration. "I mean, I already told my buddy who owns the comic book store in Bingleyton that he could have the job, and he could really use the money." He shot Fanny a pleading look with his expressive eyes, but she wasn't falling for his act this time.

"All I know is that I've heard everyone talk about how important family is in this town." She shrugged as she backed out of the door. "Seems like you could make the time if that was really the case. I know I would make the time if it were my family."

"I like her." BeeBee nodded at Fanny, then her eyes grew wide with excitement. "Hey, you should come to my baby shower. A lot of people are bringing their kids, so I'm sure you'll see some of your dance students there."

"But—but?"

"But what?" Law crossed his arms and smiled, a grin that still somehow made Fanny's heart roll over in her chest even though it had a distinct cat-with-canary-feathers-sticking-out-of-its-mouth quality.

"But of course, I will," Fanny said, then sighed. It wouldn't help Madame Rousseau or the studio if everyone thought she was a snob who turned down invitations from perfectly nice people, even if they were practically strangers. Still, this was definitely not helping her plan to avoid Law outside of their practices.

"Great!" BeeBee exclaimed before turning back to Law. "I was just teasing you about the nursery, by the way. I told Bill your friend owns the comic book store in Bingleyton and he practically did a happy dance. It was one of his favorite places as a kid when he came to the area for summer camp. Such a nerd," she added with obvious affection warming her voice. "I know you're super busy with the general contractor's license—and dancing, apparently—but if you have time, could you carve some of those engraved floating shelves like you did for Chrysta's nursery?"

"You do wood carvings?" Fanny's chin jerked back in surprise. She hadn't exactly pegged him as the creative, crafty type. When he had said earlier he was a woodworker, she assumed it was basic functional stuff like chairs and desks.

Law opened his mouth, then rubbed the back of his neck, which flushed red.

BeeBee answered for him. "He does the most amazing, artistic carvings. Custom cheese boards with intricate designs and pictures imprinted on them, furniture, even animals. Oh, you could carve my water buffaloes from the farm into the shelves!" she said, enthusiastically hitting Law on the arm as she talked.

He rubbed the side of his shoulder, then cleared his throat. "We'll, uh, go over the details later. I don't really do the woodworking thing so much anymore. It was really…time-consuming. I've moved on to greener pastures, so to speak."

Greener pastures as in more money, of course. Fanny understood the need to make a living; she had worked her fair share of side hustles from modeling dancewear to doing kids' birthday parties dressed as a fairy princess. But she never let that get in the way of her need to perform, her creative drive. The fact that Law had just given up on his own art proved he didn't only have commitment issues when it came to women. Definitely not the guy one moved to a small town in the middle of nowhere for.

"Well, I've got to get back to the studio,"

Fanny said, hooking a thumb over her shoulder at the opposite side of the street. "It was nice meeting you, BeeBee."

"Same," BeeBee replied with a wave. "I'll have Law get the details of the baby shower to you. Hey, you guys could come together."

Fanny fled out of the doorway before BeeBee came up with another way to force her into the arms of a guy who would never be able to support her in the way she needed, no matter how much she was starting to wish he would.

Worst of all, she didn't even get her soda.

CHAPTER NINE

ALTHOUGH MOST OF Crystal Hill viewed Bingleyton as their regional rival in all things from high school sports to battling for annual tourist dollars, Law had never seen the point of the enmity. He had traveled enough to know there was room for the neighboring towns to coexist peacefully. Carter Jacobsen, the owner of Double Jay's Comic Book Store in downtown Bingleyton, had been one of his best friends for over twenty years now. The pair had met at hockey camp in Lake Placid the summer before sixth grade, and despite their teams playing against each other in high school, had maintained their friendship.

Grabbing the bag of black-and-whites from Georgia's Bakery out of the passenger seat of his Jeep, Law walked around his car and opened the door to Carter's shop. "Hey, there, Sarge."

Carter had rigged the doorbell to play the theme song to *Superman*. He looked up from behind the counter and smiled when he saw Law, but his smile morphed into a look of panic when he saw the bag in Law's hands.

"Jeez Louise, man." He looked around the shop as he rushed past the counter before snatching the bag away and hiding it behind a large Hulk figurine. "We talked about this last time. If anyone in town saw me with Crystal Hill contraband, I'd be out of business in a week. Nondescript packaging only." Peering out the window, he opened the bag and inhaled deeply before relocating it to a shelf beneath the cash register.

"Aren't you volunteer firefighters supposed to be like brave superheroes?" Law teased, leaning his elbows on the counter. After a stint in the National Guard, Carter continued to serve as a local volunteer firefighter, earning the nickname "Sarge" from those closest to him. "You rescued a puppy from a raging wildfire in California, but you're afraid of the octogenarian owner of Nana's Little Bakeshop next door?"

"First of all, I'd walk through a thousand fires for Smaug," Carter said. He nodded at the boxer puppy snoring contentedly from a velvet beanbag in the corner of the shop. "Second of all, Nana is my grandmother's best friend and, darn skippy, I'm scared of her! Between the two of them, they know where all the bodies are buried in this town and that's optimistically a euphemism. You don't mess with the town elders of Bingleyton."

"That sounds like the women of Crystal Hill." Law snorted. He drummed on the countertop with both hands and turned to survey the shop. It was a two-level store with a winding staircase that led to the upper floor where the rare vintage and collector's edition comics were stored. The first floor had open racks of books in the center for people to page through and action figures on low shelves where kids could play with them without being scolded. Carter's family had owned the shop for decades, but once Carter had taken over after his grandfather's death, he had renovated the whole place and business had really taken off.

"Speaking of which, I've got someone coming to help with the store next week," Carter said. He surreptitiously reached into the hidden bag and pulled out a cookie, taking an enormous bite and chewing it with relish before continuing. "So if your cousin can have the room cleared out that she wants to use for the nursery, I can probably get most of the work done then."

Law swiveled back around and nodded. "That would be awesome. BeeBee's chomping at the bit to get it done, so I really appreciate you subbing in for me. My life is just so crazy right now between applying for my general contractor's license and trying to get the permits so I can get going on the foundation for my own place." Guilt gnawed at his insides and he shoved his right hand inside the pocket of his hoodie to keep his twitching fingers hidden.

"I'm happy to do it," Carter replied, brushing crumbs off his plaid button-down, which Law knew covered a Superman T-shirt. His friend bore an uncanny resemblance to the late Christopher Reeves and leaned into the likeness with gusto. "You sacrificed your weekends last year to help with the renovations to this place." He gestured to the bright blue walls and copper light fixtures in the shop. "I'm happy to return the favor. Just remember to keep my involvement on the down-low. The fewer people who know I'm doing this for a Crystal Hillite, the better."

"That shouldn't be an issue," Law said. Bee-Bee was the only one around the house during the day, and even though she had begrudgingly agreed to let someone from Bingleyton do the work, she wasn't likely to go spreading that information around town.

"Great," Carter said. He adjusted his glasses

on his nose as the doorbell sounded again. Raising his hand in a wave, he greeted the customer entering behind Law. "Mr. Napolitano, how's it going?"

Law twisted around to see a tall man with dark hair and a very obvious spray tan.

The man raised a glass bottle filled with thick green liquid in a return of the salute. "Can't complain. Business is up and my body fat is below seven percent. Just came in to look for a birthday present for my nephew."

Carter nodded at the man and said to Law, "Napolitano Fitness is one of the fastest growing gyms in the region. They just opened up a second location in Bath."

"And looking to expand even further," the man said. He walked over to stand next to Law and picked up a Hulk figure. Checking the price tag on Hulk's feet, he frowned and set it back down before giving Law a once-over. "You look like you work out, young man. Here—" He dug around in the pocket of his extremely tight jeans before producing a card. "Have a punch card, good for a free personal training session at any of our two, soon to be three, locations in the area."

"Where's the third going to be?" Carter asked.

"We're in talks to acquire a space in Crystal

Hill," Mr. Napolitano replied. He squatted with some difficulty and grabbed a pack of Pokemon cards from below the counter. "This should do the trick."

Carter took the pack and moved to the cash register to ring it up. "How old is your nephew going to be?" He took the credit card Mr. Napolitano offered.

"Five...or ten, somewhere in there," Mr. Napolitano said absently. "It's hard to keep track. Anyway, we've got the perfect space lined up if we can get the owner of the building to make up her mind on selling. It's an old theater with a dance studio attached next door. Most of it will be a complete gut job, right down to the studs, but we should be able to keep some of the studio space for Pilates classes. The folks coming in from the city for the summer love those."

Law's stomach churned as uneasily as if he had drunk the liquid sludge Mr. Napolitano was swigging. If the dance studio disappeared, Fanny wouldn't ever have a reason to come back to Crystal Hill, let alone even consider staying there for good. It hit him suddenly how much he wanted that connection to remain uncut.

"Well, Law here is an amazing builder and should have his general contractor's license by the time you're ready to start demo-ing,"

Carter said as he bagged the Pokemon cards and handed them to Mr. Napolitano. "He's local too, so he'd be cheaper than paying someone from out of town."

Mr. Napolitano's dark eyes brightened at the word *cheap*.

"Well, then—" he tapped the punch card in Law's hand "—our head office number is on the card. Give us a buzz when you've got your license and we can start talking numbers." He took a long drink from his bottle, then raised it once more at Carter. "Always glad to help out the next generation of entrepreneurs. Keep hustling, boys."

After the door to the shop closed, Law turned the card over in his hand and looked over his shoulder at Mr. Napolitano's departing Mercedes Benz. "Do you think he'll really try to open a location in Crystal Hill?"

"Oh, yeah," Carter said. "The tan and the hair plugs are fake, but when it comes to business, he's legit. He's a cheapskate, even though he's loaded, so if you put in a bid for the job with a lower rate you'll probably get it. You don't mind me putting your name in, right? With your skills, it won't take long for them to approve your GC license and get your business going."

Law shook his head. "No, I appreciate it. I

guess I'm just overwhelmed with everything going on right now." He tucked the card in the pocket of his shorts and squinted at the clock over Carter's head. "Shoot, is it really four thirty already? I've got to get going."

"I'll see you next week," Carter said as Law waved once and made quickly for the door. "Thanks for the cookies."

Law's mind spun as fast as the tires on his Jeep as he raced back to Crystal Hill. Landing a job as big as the one Mr. Napolitano had dangled would be a huge boon for a brand-new contractor's business. He'd be a fool to turn it down. On the other hand, if Madame Rousseau was thinking about retiring, maybe Fanny would consider taking over in her stead. He caught a glimpse of the hopeful way his eyes lit up in the rearview mirror and shook his head. What was wrong with him? Fanny was very clear in the fact that she didn't want to date him. When he ran into her at Mama Renata's two days ago, it seemed like she couldn't get away from him fast enough. Harboring a crush on a woman intent on leaving town and sacrificing a potentially lucrative opportunity on the off chance she might consider staying seemed like a spectacularly bad idea. Yet when he made it to the studio on time and completed the box step correctly on the first try, her pleased smile felt like the first rays of sunshine in spring after years of winter.

"You've been practicing," she said, tapping her phone to stop the music after the first refrain.

"A little, here and there." He shrugged and avoided her gaze as she seemed to have X-ray vision when it came to half-truths. The whole truth was that he had been practicing the steps from the audition so much he could have sworn he was dancing in his sleep.

"Good," she said. "Because we're recording the first eight-counts today and sending them to Keith and Collette. Since you've got the box step down, maybe we can even add on another move before we record?" She phrased it like a question, but Law was beginning to catch on that when her voice went up an octave, it was more of a command. A command he'd happily follow as long as she kept smiling at him like that.

"Let's do this!" He clapped his hands together twice.

She cringed and rubbed her temples. "What if we did this more quietly?" Closing her eyes, Fanny shook her head. "I'm sorry. I didn't sleep much last night. There's a leak in the pipes and water started dripping into my room from the bathroom last night. I plugged it with towels, but I still spent half the night moving my stuff off the floor so it didn't get ruined if the water spread."

"After we're done here, I'll take a look at it," Law offered.

"You really don't have to," Fanny said. "I'm taking enough of your time already. Let's get back to work. Now the next thing after the box step is simple." She assumed their dance frame once again with Law's right hand on her waist and his left hand in hers stretched out to the side. "So, you're going to turn your body to face the mirror, but keep your hips parallel to mine. Like this." She twisted her torso like a corkscrew and turned her face and chest to the mirror. "Now keeping your body in this position, take two steps forward starting with your left foot."

"Erm." So many directions for one body to go in all at once. Law felt like a computer on to which someone had just spilled a Super Big Gulp Slurpee, something that may or may not have happened to him. Twice. "I turn my body." He twisted like she showed him, every muscle in his back protesting the unnatural stretch.

"It will help if you hold me tighter," she said, pressing her own hand more firmly into his back. "It's less of a strain on your core, especially if you're not super flexible."

He cleared his throat. "Like this?" Using the right arm that was curled behind her back, he tightened his grip and pulled her against him. Their hips were barely "showing daylight" as the school guidance counselors had always advised the couples in high school who got a little too cozy against the lockers. His back did feel looser and he was able to turn his chest to the mirror as she showed him; unfortunately, it also put a strain on his injured wrist, sending pins and needles through his arm. Gritting his teeth, he ignored the pain.

"Good." She nodded. "When you're ready, walk forward. Ready? Left foot, right foot and together."

He followed her instructions. Swiping glances down at his feet, he also noticed his hips drifting away from hers. "Gah! Why did I move to the side?"

"Because your eyes and head moved down and toward me," Fanny said, breaking their frame and wiping her forehead with the sleeve of her plum-colored leotard. "Dance is a study of contradictions in movement. When your head goes one way, your body will go another to balance it out."

"And here I thought I was in charge," he muttered, backing up to where they had started.

"Let's try again," Fanny said. "This time, eyes in the mirror. Listen to my voice."

He assumed their frame with one hand on her back holding her lower body close and the other extended toward the mirror with her hand in his. Turning his body, he forced his eyes to focus on their reflection. Law wasn't the type of guy who typically spent a lot of time looking in a mirror, yet the image of him and Fanny embracing was a picture he could have stared at for hours. The contrast of her gleaming dark hair with his sandy waves, the way his rugged tan from hours spent outdoors made her ivory skin almost glow. She had been right. The balance of their contradictions was what made them look so great together.

Her voice startled him out of his Narcissus-like trance. "Ready to walk? Five, six, seven, eight, walk left, right, together and turn your body back toward mine." Her voice moved in the same rhythm as her body and it made it easier for even a graceless oaf like him to follow along as he untwisted his body toward hers once more, his hand continuing to grasp her tightly despite the electric shots of pain.

"All right," Fanny said. She cleared her throat

and stepped back, taking her phone out of the pocket of her skirt. She cleared her throat and rubbed her hip with one hand. "Now we'll put the whole thing together with music and then record."

"Oh, right." For a second, Law had forgotten they were doing this for another couple. When she was in his arms, it felt like the rest of the world, all his worries and other people's demands on his time—it all melted away. "Yes, I'm ready. To, um, record."

Because as much as he liked the image of him and Fanny dancing together at a wedding, he still wasn't ready for forever. His house was still just a bunch of loosely arranged pavers, his business even less set in stone. But something in him whispered that the longer he spent with Fanny in his arms, the harder it would be to imagine himself with anyone else as his partner. On the dance floor and in life.

The only question was, what would get an incredible, worldly woman like Fanny to stay in a little town like Crystal Hill for her next act in life? He might not have much to offer personally, but his town might just seal the deal.

CHAPTER TEN

FANNY WAS NOT easily impressed, yet the way Law had taken her admittedly harsh criticism, worked on the steps and performed them today had her impressed. After the last session, she hadn't been sure they would have anything to record for Keith and Collette and now they had almost three eight-counts.

"Before I hit Record, can we try adding on to the intro?" she asked Law as she took a swig from her water bottle. His nose wrinkled in the way that suggested he was already starting to doubt himself and she quickly added, "I'm not asking anything more of you. To fill in the music, I just want to have the bride walk around the groom once. It's a moment for the bride to show off her dress and a moment for the groom to show off his bride."

"You're the boss, Fannantha," Law joked. "So I stand in my spot and gaze adoringly at you as you walk around me."

"Now you're getting it." She laughed and held up one finger. "The choreography, of course. Not my name. Your attempts at guessing, by the way, are getting more absurd by the minute."

Law walked to his spot in the center of the studio and put his left hand to his invisible tuxedo jacket. "One of these days," he said as Fanny set her phone on the tripod to record and hit Play on the music.

Imagining she wore a voluminous wedding dress, she kept a wide enough space for the theoretical skirt to billow as she circled him. Following her instruction, Law's eyes followed her with an almost worshipful intent. She found herself struggling to concentrate on following the beat of the introductory music, her heart was thundering so loud in her ears. Why was he able to do that to her with just one look? Marshaling every ounce of her well-trained focus, she hit her mark as he reached out his right hand and spun her into him. She counted out loud for the box step, giving him time to match his steps to hers.

"Now twist your body and walk two, three, together," she said in time to the music. "Eyes up, Lawson," she reminded him as they faced each other again. "Remember, if your eyes go down, your head goes down and your hips go the other way. A newlywed couple wants to stay close together, right?"

"Right," he breathed, a blush flooding his cheeks. "If we were in love, that's exactly what we would want to do."

"Okay," she said. "Let's do it one more time and then we can be done."

"Oh." His face fell and he rubbed the back of his neck. "That's it for today, then? That was fast."

"Well, I don't want to throw too much at Keith this first session," she said. "This is already more than I had planned, but you're catching on so quickly I figured we'd take the puck and run with it, to use your vernacular."

He chuckled and shook his head. "Not even close, but it's cute when you try."

The corners of her lips turned up on their own at him calling her cute and Fanny forced them down into the stern expression she used for her middle school hip-hop class. "Enough playing around. One more time."

They recorded it again. This time, Fanny talked through the steps as they did them, in hopes it would remind her that that this was a job, like any other, and not rehearsal for her own wedding to a man who was far too handsome to be safe. After they were done, she started to put her things away into her bag, but when she hefted it over her shoulder and exited through the door, she saw Lawson heading up the stairs to her apartment.

"Um, you're going the wrong way," she said, pointing to the stairs leading down to the street exit. "Out is that way."

He pointed the opposite direction. "I'm fixing the leak in your bathroom," he said matter-of-factly. "Remember?"

Oh, come on. How was she supposed to quell the flutters in her heart every time he looked at her when he was apparently bent on invading more than her dance space? "I can't pay you, just so you know," she said to his back as he tromped up the stairs. "All the green in my pasture is being saved for wherever I end up after I figure out my next purpose in life."

He waved a hand over his shoulder. "This one's a freebie," Law called as he opened the door to her little apartment.

Fanny practically jogged up the stairs to catch up with him. "I'm normally very neat," she said, in response to the clothes piled on top of the bed. "I didn't want my stuff to get wet in case the leak spread. There's not a whole lot of storage space in here."

"I share a small trailer with all my tools and

handyman supplies." Law quirked a half smile at her. "You won't get any judgment from me." He pointed at the small door to the right. "Bathroom?"

"Yup."

Fanny watched as he opened the small cabinet under the sink and examined the pipes. When he emerged, he withdrew a wad of damp, colorful T-shirts. "These yours?"

"Yeah." She folded her arms over her chest. "Those are my tour shirts. I collected one from every tour I went on with a musical or ballet company. I used them to stop the leak."

He pulled one out and scanned the list of locations from the tour of *Carousel*. "Hey, I was in Denver in 2023, too."

"Really?" She walked toward him and peeked over his shoulder at the shirt. "That's funny. What month?"

"December," he said, handing the shirt to her. "I was there to teach snowboarding at a resort in the Rockies."

"Our tour was there until the end of November," she said. "Funny."

He pulled another out and held it in front of him. "Sweet Charity," he read out loud. "I dated a girl named Charity once. It, uh, didn't end well."

"Shocker," she said wryly. "Let me guess, it was you, not her?"

"Oh, no, it was definitely her," he quipped. "She used to call me at three in the morning to tell me what she thought we should name our kids. Two weeks into dating."

"I don't believe you." Fanny widened her eyes and shook her head. "No one would do that."

"No way!" Law looked back at her with an expression of disbelief. "I was in Seattle the same year as you! The band I was in at the time had a gig out there in July."

"I was there in August," Fanny said. The bathroom was small as it was, but it suddenly felt even smaller. She swallowed and grabbed the shirt out of his hands. "Maybe I should just take all of these—"

Before she could reach for the rest of the stack, he had pulled out two more and spread them over the sink to run his finger down the list of theaters. "This is crazy. I was in Boston the same year as you for a gong ringer's convention. Yes, there was a girl involved." He held up one hand without lifting his eyes to her. "Holy moly, when you were in Tokyo with the ballet company, I was there, too."

"And what lifelong calling were you chasing then?" she teased.

He narrowed his eyes and muttered, "I mean, the guys at Benihana made hibachi look so cool." Shaking his head, he turned to face her and gestured with a shirt in each hand. "Don't you think this is wild? All the places we've traveled to, and so many times we just missed each other. Not that I'm one of those people who think their life is controlled by destiny or fate or anything like that. I just think it's cool that we both ended up here in Crystal Hill." He looked down as he balled the shirt in his hands. "You know, out of all the places I traveled, I realized that this town is special. Do you think that maybe both of our winding trails leading us back to this place might mean that your next calling could be here?"

Fanny leaned back against the door, clutching the shirt she had taken from him. "It's just a coincidence." It had to be. "For once I agree with you. I don't believe in destiny either." She believed in chasing after what you wanted, in pursuing your goal with singular determination. Anything else felt like cheating.

So why was there something about Law that made her want to believe in a little magic?

"Just saying that if you take a walk around town, you might be surprised by how inspired you get." His eyes fell to her lips and he swallowed hard, his chest moving up and down as though the air had become thin for him as well. "Fanny, there's something I heard at the comic book store today, I think you should know. The studio—"

Just then, the pipe below the sink burst, a spray of water hitting Law at the knees. He yelped and jumped back, dropping the shirts in alarm. Watching him dive back in to fix a problem he wasn't getting paid to fix without even being asked, Fanny wondered if maybe, just maybe, she had judged him a little too harshly.

The next day, the apartment still smelled faintly of damp cotton, so she went for a walk around the lake to get some fresh air. The afternoon was overcast and still chilly enough that Fanny needed a sweatshirt over her T-shirt and leggings. She actually didn't mind the thick clouds darkening in the distance. A clear, sunny sky wouldn't have matched her state of mind, which was growing cloudier by the minute. Church bells rang from the chapel on the next block over from the bed-and-breakfast, and the slightly melancholy clang was such a perfect soundtrack to her walk that she took her earbuds out of her ears and tucked them in her pocket. A little music would help drown out Law's words that had echoed in her head since last night:

"Do you think that maybe both of our winding trails leading us back to this place might mean that your next calling could be here?"

IT WAS THE first week in April now. She had a little over a month before the recital, at which time she would be free of her obligation in Crystal Hill and off to her next grand adventure. Trouble was, she had no idea what that adventure was going to be or where it would lead her. At least once she got paid for Collette and Keith's wedding dance sessions, she would have enough money to support herself while she embarked on the second act of her professional life. Her future was wide-open and full of possibility.

So why did she feel like a door had closed behind her and locked her in a small, windowless room?

In the stillness after the last echo of the bells had fallen to silence, Fanny's phone rang. It was Collette.

"Hi, girl," Fanny said as she followed the trail into the forest of pine trees. "Can you hear me okay? This town is out in the middle of nowhere and the reception tends to be a bit spotty anytime you venture away from the main street."

"I can hear you fine," Collette replied, construction noise and an ambulance siren follow-

grueling performance. That thought reminded her that she had ordered an Italian soda from Mama Renata's, which was waiting for her to pick up, and she doubled back around in anticipation. As the main town square came back into view, she had to admit it was one of the prettiest places she had ever seen, a blend of European charm and the welcoming spirit that was so distinctly American. It was like someone had taken a bit of every different corner of the world and deposited in beneath the beautiful mountaintops guarding the small hamlet. So many different people from different places had come together to make this their home and she understood why.

Still, no matter how charming a place and its people—one in particular—were, charm alone would never be enough. She needed something that would fulfill her, a purpose with its own challenges and triumphs. That seemed like an awfully big ask from a town so small.

CHAPTER ELEVEN

LAW WAS NEVER the type of person who believed in fate with a capital *F*.

As he adjusted the pavers on the foundation at his house yet again—paying for the lawyer to help set up his business was going to cost him exactly one extra bedroom—he reflected on the way he had always sort of drifted from one hobby, one girl, one place to the next when he got bored with the last one, trusting the Universe to sort things out however it saw fit. Much like his favorite breakfast sausage at Big Joe's Diner, he didn't need to know how it all came to be.

But he hadn't been able to sleep last night, thinking about Fanny and their parallel journeys over the past several years. More than once—more than twice—they had been in the same city at almost the exact same time. This wasn't some random coincidence, just like the way he felt about her wasn't some everyday crush. He had never looked forward to scheduled obligations and yet he found himself counting down the hours each day until their practice sessions together. And it wasn't just because holding her in his arms brought a thrill no mountain peak or jousting tournament had ever brought him. It was because he couldn't wait to hear what she had to say to him that day, even if it was a sarcastic retort to his latest attempt to guess her name. Being around Fanny was challenging, exciting. Most of all, she was fun.

And when he stood and turned around, she was also standing in the spot where his front porch would be.

Law jumped back, wondering if he had actually started thinking about her so much that he was hallucinating her like some desert mirage. "Fannetta, what are you doing here?"

She stepped over the pavers and into his theoretical mudroom. With her hands on her hips, she turned in a small circle and surveyed the foundation. "I needed to talk to you. Wasn't your house bigger last time?"

"Ironically, starting my own business is turning out to be very expensive," Law said, cringing at the number a website designer had quoted him over email yesterday. "I had to cut some corners. Literally, because corners are actually the most expensive part of a house design."

"That's interesting," she said thoughtfully. "I know next to nothing about building or even owning a house. Although, to be fair, I've been living out of suitcases for the last ten-plus years."

Law dusted his hands off on his jeans and walked across his "kitchen" to stand next to her. "So, what did you need to talk to me about?"

Her eyes lit up like a beam of sunlight piercing a forest. "It's about our dance." She pulled her phone out of her purse and held it up. "I just got this email from Collette and Keith's wedding planner. He wants to join the Zoom practice session we've scheduled with them for this Friday." Tucking the phone back in her bag, she looked back up at him. "It's really important that we impress him. He already fired one choreographer and while I don't think they have time to hire someone else, I can't afford to lose this job."

"Whatever you need me to do, I'm in," Law said, spreading his arms out.

"I'm glad you said that because I want to add a lift to the dance," she announced.

"A lift?" Law's hand twitched reflexively as he dropped it to his side before hiding it in his pocket. With the other hand, he pushed his hair off his forehead, which was starting to sweat. "What—what kind of lift?"

"Oh, nothing too complicated." She waved her hand in front of her face as if she could shoo away his doubt like a pesky mosquito. "I mean, Keith has to be able to do it, too. But it still has to look cool enough so the wedding planner keeps me on. Also, we have to start practicing right away for it to be perfect by Friday." She stepped past him into the open space that was meant to be the living room. "There should be enough room here. Some bay windows looking out over the field would be perfect for this room, by the way."

He had actually planned on bay windows if he could still afford them by the time he got to building. But right now he had more immediate concerns than architectural details. Concerns like whether or not his injury would allow him to lift Fanny without even the slightest chance he might drop her or hurt her. "Are you sure we need a lift in the dance?" He followed her into the "living room" hesitantly. "What if we just did some more of the cha-cha-cha moves from the audition? I've been practicing them just in case you put them in and I think I've actually got the rhythm down." He demonstrated for her, watching her face desperately for a sign of approval.

She smiled and his hopes lifted. "No."

"No, we're not going to do it, or no, I don't have the rhythm down?"

"Yes to both."

He sighed. "I'm in my thirties now." Waving a hand up and down his body, he grimaced. "There's been wear and tear. Hockey sticks to the kidneys. My joints make unholy noises first thing in the morning now. Some old injuries, some more recent. I don't want to sound like I'm making excuses, but I also want to make sure you're not putting too much faith in my abilities here."

She walked over to him and put a hand on his elbow. "Law, I promise you can do this. I've worked with dozens of partners over the years, guys and girls. Lifts are about sharing weight, not one person muscling through and doing all the work. How about we give it a try before you decide that you can't do it?"

His chin shot up. It was eerie the way she could read his mind, almost as eerie as the way their lives had been leading them toward each other throughout their travel. "Okay."

"All right." She rubbed her hands together.

"So, the last thing we did was the walk, walk, together and face each other, yes?"

He nodded and forced his hand out of his pocket to assume their dance frame. "We ended here."

"Your posture is improving," she said with a pleased glow in her cheeks. "Next, we're going to take a step back to pull apart, but keep holding hands."

He followed her instructions, clutching her hands in his as if he could will his nerves to behave. "Got it."

"Now we come back together, but side by side," she said as she stepped back toward him with the right side of her body parallel, brushing against his left, their cheeks a breath apart as if she had gone in to kiss him and just missed him. "Now step back and apart again, keep holding my hands and then step toward my other side." They repeated the step again on the other side.

"This reminds me of playing London Bridge on the playground when I was a kid," he turned his head and said softly in her ear.

"If you start singing 'My Fair Fanny,' I'm out of here," she laughed. "Now you're going to wrap your right arm around my waist," she said as she took his arm and physically placed it around her. "And what I want you to do is basically hold me on your hip and walk in a circle."

He bent his head to look her directly in the eyes. "Fanngelica, I'm not comfortable hoisting you like I'm holding a bag of groceries in one hand and opening the door with my other." Law bit his lip and confessed at least a part of what worried him. "What if I drop you?"

"You won't," she said. "Because I'm going to jump as you lift so the work isn't all on you. Okay, we're going to bend our knees one, two, then you lift on three. Got it?"

"You make it seem so easy."

"As easy as counting to three. Ready? Bend one, two, lift."

He bent his knees then tightened his grip as she jumped. She was right—it was a lot easier than he had thought. Instead of a dead lift, it was more a question of balancing her against his hip as he walked. Pivoting slowly, one foot then the other, he turned his head to look up at her silhouetted against the horizon, an angel captured midflight. But the motion stretched some muscle in his arm that sent an unexpected zap of pain, and suddenly his grip weakened. Before he could complete the circle of steps, he quickly bent his knees and set her down.

She put her hands on her hips and shook her head. "Why did you stop?"

Law rubbed his arm. "I had a...a muscle spasm in my arm and I didn't want you to get hurt. I have an...old injury there." Six months was considered aged for cheese. Probably for injuries too, right? He didn't want to drop her, and he also didn't want her to drop him as a partner if she thought he was weak.

"Or you had already decided that you couldn't do it before we even got to the lift and your body responded the way your mind directed it to," she shot back, blowing a loose strand of hair out of her face. "I appreciate you trying to protect me, but I'm a trained dancer. I know how to come out of a simple lift."

Her face was flushed, and the way her dark eyebrows furrowed together, he could tell she was frustrated and trying not to lose it. Seemed like he had struck more nerves than the one in his hand. "I'm sorry, but I don't feel confident enough to lift you with just one hand. Isn't there another move that will do the trick?"

"Look, Lawson." She stepped toward him again, gazing up at him with clear-eyed intensity as if trying to make him see something apparent to only her. "I get that all of this is new to you. If you're not comfortable with a one-handed lift, we can modify it and use two hands. All I need you to do is try your best. If it doesn't work, we try again and if that doesn't work, then we can pivot. No one gets everything perfect on the first try, right?"

All his life experiences stood in contradiction to that statement. He opened his mouth to say just that, then shut it again. Maybe everything in life had come so easily to him because he never actually tried anything out of his comfort zone before now. Maybe she was right about him giving up before he had even begun. He took a deep breath. "Let's try a two-handed lift. I think—I know I can do that."

"What if we try this?" She moved even closer into him, putting her right hand in his left. "Put your right arm around my waist and scoop up my legs. Then all you have to do is lift and turn. Okay?"

"Lift and turn," Law repeated. "I can do that."

"On the count of three," she said. "And a one, and a two, and a three."

On three, she leaned into him as he reached beneath her knees and tucked her against his chest, holding her as carefully as if she were a box filled with Mrs. Van Ressler's prized Murano glass figurines. When he set her down, she crossed her legs and twirled under his arm so effortlessly it looked like they had been doing the move for years.

"Wow," he murmured, still holding her close, yet unable to let her go. The bundle of feelings that arose—accomplishment, pride, awe at what she could help him to do—it was too exhilarating to relinquish. "I can't believe we just did that."

"And it will be even easier in the studio," she replied, her voice sounding a little breathless. He didn't blame her for being surprised; he was in actual shock that he could pull off something so graceful. "Your heels will be able to swivel better on a firmer surface."

"Why aren't we doing this in the studio today?" he asked, finally and reluctantly let her go.

"The studio isn't available today," she said, shielding her eyes from the sun as a gust of wind moved the clouds away that had been blocking its rays. "Madame Rousseau was having some guy come over to do an inspection of the building. I guess she's trying to get ahead of any other problems like the pipe that burst in my bathroom. He should be done by this evening, but I'm teaching all night tonight. You're still coming for our regularly scheduled session tomorrow, right?"

The puzzle pieces clicked into place all at once. If Madame Rousseau was having an inspection done, she was probably serious about selling the place. On the one hand, the sooner she put it up for sale, the more likely the buyer would be Napolitano. If Law hustled on his paperwork and gathering a crew, he could have everything in place to start the job as soon as the ink was dry on the escrow papers. However, that would mean no more dance studio. No more dance studio meant no more Fanny. His heart froze with panic at that thought and he reached for her hand as she took out her phone.

"I think I know why Madame Rousseau is having an inspection done," he said. "I heard something about the building the other day."

"It's a beautiful building, isn't it?" she said, scrolling down her calendar with one long finger. "I love the look of the classic theaters from the turn of the century. To have that attached to the studio is so rare. It's such a great resource for the town, especially since it's such a far drive to the city where the major dance companies and theater groups perform. If I won the lottery, I would buy a place exactly like this one—oh, shoot." Fanny's face fell as her finger stilled. "I'll have to postpone my call with my life coach if we're going to do the Zoom on

Friday." She turned and walked quickly back to her car. "I've got to head back and reschedule that ASAP or she'll charge me for the missed session. See you tomorrow, Law."

"But—I...oh, well." There would be another time to tell her about the potential sale. Besides, there was always a chance he would tell her and it wouldn't make a difference to her. She had never explicitly said she wanted to stay here and take over for Madame Rousseau, even though her last statement caused a bubble of hope to form in his head and whisper, "There's a chance." Someone had to win the lottery, right?

For now, it was probably better if he hedged his bets, continuing to dance with her while preparing his business in case the sale to Napolitano was a done deal. Law didn't leave anything to fate, chance or the New York State Lottery system.

Despite having it all sorted out, Law couldn't shake the uneasy suspicion that something still wasn't quite right. He convinced himself it was because he had been spending far too much time lately with his brother, Lucas. Lucas was unfailingly honest. Unshakably honest. Annoyingly honest to the point of contagion, because when they got together that evening at the cheese shop to go over the application for Law's general contractor's license, he found himself spilling the beans about the potential sale of the studio and his dilemma about whether or not to tell Fanny.

Lucas listened thoughtfully as he pulled balls of buffalo mozzarella out of their saltwater bath and placed them on a tray as Law told him everything from the trip to the comic book store to the exploding pipe and the T-shirts, all the way to the issues with the lift. After he had finished, Law threw up his hands and pulled a stool out from under the stainless steel countertop. "So, what do you think I should do?" he asked, sitting and reaching for one of the fresh balls of cheese still warm from the bath.

"First of all, you can get your dirty paws off my cheese," Lucas said. He slapped Law's hand away with a pair of latex gloves, then handed them to Law. "You know the cheese lab rules. No glove, no grub."

Law rolled his eyes. "You know, I thought fatherhood had mellowed you, but apparently not."

"If anything, becoming a parent has made me more paranoid about bacteria," Lucas responded. He opened the fridge next to the counter and bent his head with a stern scowl as he surveyed the contents. "A single listeria microbe could send my baby girl to the emergency room.

Can you put the gloves on and cover the mozzarella with plastic wrap while I move some things around in here to make space?"

"No problem." Law snapped the gloves over his hands and reached for the box of plastic wrap on the shelf over the sink. He continued to talk as he stretched the sticky material over the entire tray of cheese. "I just feel bad not telling Fanny everything I know about the potential sale, but if I tell her and the sale doesn't go through, I've just cost myself a huge job for a woman who might not even be here two months from now. She could be chasing her passion for farming lemongrass in Thailand and I'd be stuck here in handyman land downsizing my foundation to the size of a doghouse."

"Wow," Lucas said after he put the tray in the fridge and closed the door, then removed his head covering. "You really want her to stay, don't you?"

"That's not at all what I said."

"Once you get married, you develop a special skill for reading subtext." Lucas gave him an insufferably smug grin. "It's survival. You've clearly got feelings for this woman or you wouldn't be spending all this time with her doing something you hate. I remember Ma had to bribe you with ricotta cookies just to get you to finish your grammar homework every night."

"Well, who in the world likes grammar?" Law grumbled defensively, removing his gloves and tossing them in the trash can as he followed Lucas out into the store. "Okay, maybe Jackie, but she read dictionaries for fun as a kid. She's an anomaly."

"Stop changing the subject." Lucas turned and pointed at him. "You always do that when you feel called out or vulnerable."

"I like the Easter decorations," Law said, nodding at the brie shaped like an egg and studded with dried fruit to look like it had been painted. "That was Chrysta's doing, wasn't it?"

"My case in point," Lucas said. "I think the first thing you need to do is be honest with yourself. If you're not ready for a real, committed relationship, then there's no point in stressing yourself out. If she's just this month's fascination—"

"Watch it." Law balled his hands into fists at his side. "I don't care that you're almost half a foot taller than me, I will knock you into that cardboard bunny over there."

"What cardboard—" Lucas whipped around to follow Law's gaze and clapped a hand over his forehead. "Dang it, she must have put that up while I was in the cheese lab. I said no bunnies." He turned back to Law with a resigned expression on his face. "Listen, if you're sure you're ready to make room for someone else—and their insanely over-the-top holiday decorations—in your life, then honesty is the key. She'll know if you're hiding something and if she finds out before you tell her, you might blow your shot with her entirely."

"Thanks, man." Law reached for his jacket from the coat rack and slipped it over his shoulders before holding up a hand in a wave. "Give Chrysta and Baby Bell a hug for me. I'll try to stop in and see you all before BeeBee's baby shower, but between the contracting business, my handyman jobs and dancing with Fanny, I barely have time to breathe these days."

"Let me know if there's anything I can do to help," Lucas said. He walked around the counter, then looked back over his shoulder with narrowed eyes. "It's like I can feel the bunny's eyes watching me wherever I go."

Law shook his head and laughed as he pushed the door open and took his keys out of his coat pocket. Lucas could joke all he wanted about the decorations, but everyone knew he would do absolutely anything for his wife and daughter. The first time Law had seen his brother and Chrysta together he knew they were meant for each other, even if they didn't realize it at the time. Lucas had been ready to give her the space he needed for his cheese shop just to make her dreams come true. But that had been a totally different situation. Lucas and Chrysta both knew Crystal Hill was their home, both of them were ready to start a family and both of them knew exactly what they wanted in life. Fanny, on the other hand, was completely consumed with finding her next purpose and it wouldn't be fair to try to convince her to stay when he was too overwhelmed with just getting through the next day's to-do list, let alone think about a future and a family.

Besides, they had only known each other a few weeks. There was no way she knew him well enough to realize he wasn't being completely aboveboard with her.

CHAPTER TWELVE

"Law, I know you're holding something back," Fanny said, pointing her phone at the speaker and turning off the music with a little more force than was necessary.

She had seen it more times than she could count from other performers, in class, in rehearsals, even during shows. Especially for dancers, investing your whole self in your work was what set that person apart from the rest of the ensemble. Audiences weren't dumb. They could always tell when a performance wasn't authentic or when the performer's mind was somewhere else. The worst part was that putting anything less than your all on stage was dangerous. A distracted or restrained partner was someone you couldn't trust.

"I—I don't know what you're talking about," Law said, glancing quickly down at his hands before meeting her eyes. "I'm just doing the steps that you're showing me."

"It's the way you're doing the steps that's the problem." She marched toward him and put his right hand on her waist, grabbing his left and thrusting it out to the side. "Your shoulders and neck are tense, your jaw is clenched, which throws off your posture, and you're looking through me, not at me. Remember, we're supposed to be in love. You're dancing like your heart is somewhere else." Fanny bit her lip and stopped talking. Those last words had sounded almost…jealous. She didn't care if he was seeing someone else and that's why he was so distant. In fact, she pretty much expected him to since she had made it very clear that she was not staying in town to become his next ex-girlfriend. "Look, whatever is going on out there—" she threw her left hand toward the window facing the street "—doesn't matter in here. The only thing that matters in here is you and me. Dancing together, that is," she added quickly before he could get the wrong idea. What was wrong with her today?

His gaze finally stopped shifting and focused directly on her. "There is something I've been meaning to tell you," Law said, taking a deep breath. "But it's not about anything out there." He mimicked her motion at the window.

"Well, whatever it is, spit it out," she said irritably. "Our time together is limited, so I'd rather you not waste any more of it."

The words echoed through the small studio, her frustration evident in the biting tone. Great. She had overcompensated for sounding like a possessive girlfriend by shifting directly into screeching harpy.

"It's about..." He paused, then shook his head. "It's the lift. I guess I'm still worried you could get hurt."

"Why does this one move worry you so much?" Fanny asked, crossing her arms over her chest. "It's not even a full revolution. You're just pivoting to face the other side and holding me up at the same time. I'm barely a foot off the ground, so I don't understand—"

"I told you I had this old injury, remember?"

She rolled her eyes. "What did you do, sprain your ankle playing junior hockey? That's adorable. I danced an entire ninety-minute ballet on a broken big toe."

"My right hand doesn't work," he blurted out desperately, throwing his hands in the air. "I had an injury last year where a machine I was working with fell over and crushed my arm. It healed, but every now and then, with certain motions, I get shooting pains through my wrist and hand, tingling, and sometimes it even goes completely numb. When we did the first lift with just one hand, it acted up again and I nearly lost my grip." He shook his head and tossed a look at her so plaintive it nearly broke Fanny's heart. "If you got hurt again and it was my fault, I'd never forgive myself. I'm—I'm sorry I didn't say something about it before." His eyes dropped to the floor as he took a step back in the direction of the door. "I completely understand if you want to find a new partner before you meet with the wedding planner tomorrow."

"Lawson, stop." She took two brisk steps to stand in front of him and grab his right hand. "I appreciate your concern, but I'm a grown woman. I'll decide how much risk I can tolerate. What I won't tolerate is you using this—" she lifted his hand in hers "—as an excuse. Now tell me about the injury."

"It was last October," he said falteringly. "I was working on a custom-carved cheese board in my workshop and the saw I was using slipped out of my grasp. It happened so fast I jerked my hand away, but the handle landed directly on my forearm. The doctor said I was lucky it was the handle and not the blade."

"What did your therapy team say about the nerve damage?" she asked, turning over his hand to examine it. "Did they say it was permanent?"

"I didn't have a rehab team." Law shrugged. "After I was out of the hospital, they recommended going to occupational therapy, but I didn't have insurance. The hospital worked out a payment plan with me for the bills and that took everything I had in my savings."

"Ah." Fanny nodded. This was a familiar story. Injuries among dancers were unbelievably common, but if you were touring, you couldn't work a full-time day job that provided insurance and new dancers weren't immediately opted in to equity-sponsored insurance. She'd seen people with toes that ended up permanently deformed from dancing on fractures. The one silver lining with her own injury was that it had happened after she'd been dancing long enough to earn her equity card. Out of all her what-ifs and lost closures, there was at least no having to wonder about whether or not she could have returned to the stage if she'd had better health care.

"So, anyway…" He cleared his throat and went on, even with his hand still in hers, "That's it. That's what I've been holding back from you. Now that it's out there, do you—do you still want to be my partner?"

The naked vulnerability in his voice was far too endearing. Fanny set his hand down at his side and forced herself to back away from him when her arms longed to reach for him and pull him close to her. "I mean, it's too late to teach anyone else on such short notice," she said, fiddling with her hair. This time, she was the one who couldn't meet his eyes. She was afraid of what she might see if she looked too closely into them—or even worse, what she might do.

"Good," he said. Running a hand through his hair, he let out a small laugh. "Because I'm actually starting to enjoy dancing. Maybe that will be my new passion, since I had to give up woodworking."

"Had to give it up?" Fanny's head jerked up. "I thought you didn't do it anymore because you weren't making enough money with it."

"Oh, no," he said. "I had a shop online that was doing gangbusters, especially after the boards I made for Lucas and Chrysta's cheese party vlog went viral. It's just that after the injury, all the intricate work involved with my carving took twice as long as before and my hand would hurt so bad the next day, I'd be basically useless. There's nothing I hate more than just sitting around waiting for something to get better."

"Oof, I know that feeling." She nodded. "I had been moving my entire life, so when I was recovering from my surgery and couldn't walk, I thought I would go crazy. If it wasn't for the physical therapists getting me out of bed, I would have used my IV to lasso the wheelchair just to get out of the room."

Law snorted. "Somehow I don't think rodeo clown should be your next passion, Faneronica."

"Hey, I did a dinner theater production of *Annie, Get Your Gun*," she shot back indignantly. "I bet I'd make a great rodeo clown. Maybe BeeBee will let me practice on one of her water buffaloes."

"If you ask BeeBee to let you lasso one of her precious babies, not even I could protect you from injury," he said, then added quietly. "As much as I would want to."

She stopped chuckling, then tossed a sidelong look at his hand. "You know, the physical therapy was a big part of me regaining the mobility that I have," Fanny said, brushing her foot along the floor in a circular movement. "Even if I can't perform professionally the way I used to, just being able to dance at all is a lifesaver for me."

"I get that," he said. "Sometimes I see a piece of gorgeous cherrywood or I get an idea for a new kind of cheese board and it's really hard not to run straight back to my workshop. I do miss it." A catch in his voice made him stop and Fanny cut in before the emotion overtook him.

"Once you get your business going, maybe you'll have the money to go for a therapy evaluation," she said gently. "The profit from one really big job might be enough to pay for a treatment that could get you back to carving the way you want to."

A strange expression crossed his face, the same tension rippling his jawline as it had earlier when he had been trying to hold back the truth about his injury. "Hey, I just remembered a move I saw at my friend's wedding a few years ago. They called it a Hollywood dip. Don't you think that would be perfect to add in here?"

"So you can be a choreographer, but I can't be a rodeo clown?" she teased, wagging her finger at him. "Sounds like a double standard to me."

He laughed out loud. "Well, you always make me laugh, Fannastasia. Maybe rodeo clown isn't so far-fetched after all."

Lacing her fingers together and leaning forward to stretch them behind her back, Fanny looked up at him. "A dip is a classic wedding move, but I like to save it for the very end of the dance. It makes for a great picture and it's easier for the photographer to get the shot if they hold it instead of going on to the next move.

We've got a lot more dancing to do before we get to the end."

"Really?" Lawson sighed. "I was kind of hoping we were close to the goal line."

"Your sports metaphors are worse than useless with me, buddy," Fanny replied as she straightened her back and released her hands. "Save them for the Zoom with Keith tomorrow. Now we've just twirled out of the lift, we're going to come back together into our dance frame, but closer this time." As he put his right arm around her waist, she took his left hand and placed it over hers on his chest. "Like this."

"That—that is close," he murmured, dipping his head down so that they were almost cheek to cheek.

She could feel his heart thundering under her hand, matching the galloping of her own. "This dance is for a couple in love, looking forward to spending the rest of their lives together," she said softly. "Usually that involves fairly close physical proximity."

"What do we do now?"

"You're going to walk forward two steps and then one step to your left," she answered, nodding down at his feet so she didn't have to look into his eyes.

"So instead of a box step, it's an L step?"

"Exactly. So on three, step forward left foot, right foot, left together."

"Um, Fanny?"

"What?" His hand clasped hers so tightly, as if she held a precious jewel he didn't want her to drop. There was something so protective in it. She couldn't remember the last time she'd felt this safe with a partner. With any man, really.

"Aren't you always telling me to look up?"

She lifted her chin and saw him giving her that pleased-with-himself grin that left her torn over whether to throttle the man...or hug him.

"And a one and a two..."

Once he had gotten the L step down and reversed it on the other side, bruising only two of her toes—which was progress—they did the entire thing with the music. As soon as she turned off the song, the silence was filled by clapping coming from the doorway.

Madame Rousseau stilled her hands to pick up her cane and walked into the studio with an approving look on her face. "That was quite good," she said, looking first from Fanny to Law then back again. "Lawson Carl, where have you been hiding your talent all these years? I'm always on the lookout for male dancers to add to our ensemble."

"There's no talent to hide." Law let go of

Fanny and gestured at her with one hand, scratching the light field of evening stubble rising on his chin with the other. "It's all Fanny. She's a wonderful teacher. I mean, if she can get me to do even basic things like this without falling, I bet she could turn every student in her class into a professional dancer."

If Fanny thought herself immune to his charm and flattery by this point, her face hadn't gotten the message because her cheeks burned at the unexpected sincerity in his voice. He wasn't schmoozing her for a date or trying to wheedle his way into ending rehearsal early. He was just…being nice. She didn't even know what to say, but fortunately, Madame Rousseau did.

"Watching you two gave me an idea," she said, tapping her chin with one finger. "I know you're only demonstrating this for Fanny's friend's wedding dance, but would you be willing to perform this at the recital in May? I think it would be such inspiration for the young men in this town to see someone like Law, an athlete, up there dancing."

Fanny and Law exchanged startled glances. It was one thing, privately dancing such an intimate piece for a couple to do at their wedding. Performing it onstage in front of an entire town was quite another thing entirely. What if everyone got the wrong idea and thought they were a couple? She planned to leave for her next adventure as soon as the recital was over. That would put Law in the position of having to explain the abrupt end to their "romance" over and over again, and while there was a certain poetic justice to that given his philandering history, he had been a big help to her over the last few weeks. She couldn't do that to him even if she wasn't still sure he had truly reformed.

"I don't know if that's going to work," Law said slowly, putting his hands together and cracking his knuckles one finger at a time. "What if I trip and fall onstage? I'm still the same klutz I always was. Dancing with Fanny would make anyone look good."

Fanny nodded as he confirmed exactly what she had thought. He hadn't changed, not really. He was still a guy who would flake out if there was even a chance it might ruin his image. You couldn't count on someone like that. "Besides, I'm not really a permanent teacher here at the studio. I don't want the kids getting too attached and thinking I'm going to be here next year when I probably won't."

Law's head whipped over his shoulder at her. "Probably?" The higher octave on the last syllable almost sounded hopeful.

He didn't actually want her to stick around, did he? Fanny had assumed that part of his fascination with her was because she was leaving soon. That was pretty much an ideal scenario for a playboy like Lawson. Temporary fun with a fixed end date. Surely the guy who couldn't even commit to a plan for his future house wasn't ready for a long-term relationship?

"It was merely a suggestion," Madame Rousseau said. "The studio is my legacy, after all, and I had visions of leaving a vibrant troupe of dancers behind when I leave, a young company performing all the great classics that require strong male dancers partnering the graceful ballerinas. I'm not sure how much time I have left for that dream to become reality, though." She finished the statement with a robust coughing fit that sounded much more dramatic than her typical rasps and wheezes.

Fanny knew Madame Rousseau well enough to only be slightly affected by the obvious guilt trip. Law's stricken expression, however, told a different story.

"Of course we can perform at the recital," he said, rushing to Madame Rousseau's side and holding her elbow in one hand to support her. "And we'll get as many of the local boys to come and watch as we can wrangle. I volunteer with the junior hockey league during the winter, so I know a lot of their parents."

"Especially the single moms," Fanny muttered wryly, then cleared her throat. "I mean, if it's really important to you, Madame Rousseau. Just keep expectations low, all right? This is barely Ballroom 101 that we're doing, not Balanchine."

"Of course, dear," Madame Rousseau said, having seemingly recovered from the consumptive fit that had racked her five seconds ago. "I think the whole idea that anyone can be taught to dance for the sheer joy of it is inspiration enough." She checked the delicate gold watch on her wrist. "Goodness, look at the time. I have an appointment I must get to. You two start thinking about costumes for your pas de deux." Fanny could have sworn she heard her old mentor chuckling the second she was out the door.

"Pas de who?" Law blinked at Fanny.

"Pas de deux," Fanny said. "It means dance for two."

"Fancy." He grinned. "I like it. Shall we pas de deux, me and you?"

She pointed at the door. "I will kick you out of my studio for one more rhyme."

"*Your* studio?" he asked, tipping his nose

down to give her a very meaningful look she didn't really understand. "Maybe in time."

"Just for that, I'm putting another lift in the dance."

She didn't, but it was because it didn't serve the choreography.

Not at all because his face took on a sad puppy-dog quality at the threat.

Besides, by the end of the evening, they had polished the moves they had enough that Fanny actually felt ready for the Zoom call by Friday evening. She set up the laptop camera in front of the mirror so they could demonstrate for Collette and Keith the same way they practiced. Fiddling with the ring light placed behind the barre, she checked her watch for the tenth time in the last five minutes. Having sent several texts to Law over the last twenty-four hours reminding him how important this was and not to be late, she knew there would be no excuses or forgiveness for being tardy. Just then, his characteristic knock sounded at the door and she suppressed a pleased smile. He was not only on time, but early for once. When she looked up, however, it wasn't merely his timeliness that took her by surprise.

Lawson Carl was not wearing a hoodie, gym shorts, or even jeans without stains on the knees.

Instead, he wore a white button-down shirt with the cuffs rolled up to his elbows, cleanly pressed black dress pants and shining black shoes. His hair was combed neatly, although it still fringed his forehead in that purposely unkempt way that added an element of roguish danger to his good looks. It was a good thing she was a trained performer who could fix her face in an instant, because otherwise there was a good chance she was half a second away from drool collecting at the side of her open mouth.

"You're...on time," she said, quickly recovering from the shock of him appearing at her door and looking for all the world like a reincarnation of Cary Grant.

"Actually, I'm early," he corrected her, pointing up with his right hand at the clock hanging on the wall. Walking—no, *strutting*—into the room, he ran his hands up and down next to his body. "And dressed to the nines, might I add."

She tipped her head to one side. "Huh. Is that different from what you normally wear? I hadn't noticed."

The way his face fell made all the effort to contain the champagne-bubble feeling in her heart worth it. In fact, his expression was so crestfallen that she finally took pity on him and rolled her eyes.

"I'm kidding." She waved a hand at him. "Of course I noticed. Just so you know, when Madame Rousseau said to start thinking about costumes, she meant for the recital in over a month. We've got time to workshop ideas."

"I knew that," he said. He walked toward her, dropping the exaggerated model walk to reach her side. "But I could tell this was important to you, so I wanted to make sure I put my best foot forward. And I mean that metaphorically, because as you know, I have no best foot. They're both equally terrible."

She looked up at him, as if really seeing him for the first time. "You got all dressed up just to make me look good for the wedding planner?" It was a small gesture and yet it meant so much that he went to the effort for her without any agenda of his own. The selflessness was so incongruous with the picture she had painted of him. For her talk with the life coach next week, she would have to make sure not to list "good judge of character" as one of her attributes.

"I did." He nodded, picking up one foot like a flamingo. "I even scuffed the bottom of these shoes on the sidewalk so they wouldn't be slippery. Lucas's buddy, Bill, told me to do that since he learned the hard way at his own wedding that these things are like ice skates if you haven't roughed up the soles."

Fanny laughed. "Something tells me you'd be even more comfortable in ice skates."

"If you stick around for Crystal Hill at Christmas, you'll find out." He gave her a wink. "Behind the rec center, there's a space we turn into a public ice rink. They put twinkly lights around it and there's a hot cocoa and cider stand. It's one of my favorite things the town does during the holiday."

"Why is that?" Fanny poked him in the chest, the smell of fresh-cut grass rising from him making her suddenly aware of how close they were standing. "Because you strategically place mistletoe in various places and hang around waiting for cute girls to pass by?"

"No," he replied. The ring light behind her caught the mischievous sparkle in his light blue eyes and grew it into a golden warmth. "Because it's the time of year when you feel like a kid again. When magic seems real enough to make anything you wish for come true."

This time Fanny couldn't control the smile that spread across her face. "I love Christmas, too. The second the first frost hits, it makes me think of the first *Nutcracker* rehearsals of the year. No matter how many years I hear the same Tchaikovsky music, I never get tired of it. Seeing *The Nutcracker* as a little girl was what made me want to be a dancer."

The happy memories now held a slight bitterness, the joy tinged with the loss of holiday shows she would never get to perform.

Law reached out and took her hand in his. "Are you okay?"

She nodded, swallowing back the bitter taste until it disappeared just like her career had. "Fine. Just hard to think about my dancing days, that's all."

"You know, the studio usually does a Christmas program, but they haven't done *The Nutcracker* since you were here last time," he said gently, skating his thumb across the top of her hand and looking down at their entwined fingers. "Maybe if you—"

An alarm went off on her phone. "It's almost time for our Zoom call," she said, swiping a hand across her eyes. She cleared her throat and brushed her hands against her filmy skirt. "How do *I* look?"

His smile made his eyes crinkle at the corners and she could have sworn the music started playing even though she hadn't pressed Play. "You look perfect, Fannanda," he said softly.

She ignored his worst guess yet as she walked

over to the laptop and cued it up for the meeting to start. Within minutes, Keith and Collette joined, their faces filling one box and the wedding planner soon after. Murray Fiorino had thick, jet-black hair and eyebrows without so much as a single gray hair, despite Fanny knowing he was in his early sixties. He had coordinated some of the biggest celebrity weddings over the last thirty years and was known as much for his impeccable taste as he was for his outrageous fees. He gave a polite nod as they exchanged pleasantries.

"Collette told me about your idea to recruit a nondancer as your partner so you could gauge whether or not Keith would be able to perform the moves, is that correct?" Murray asked, lowering his steel-rimmed glasses to narrow his eyes at Law.

Fanny looked over her shoulder at Law's expression, which was a smile that appeared to have frozen on his face like a computer that stalled mid-image. She turned back around and inched to her right to block him from view so he could reboot. "Yes, that's right." She nodded, lowering her voice from the nervous squeak it had been. "Since we have to do our rehearsals long-distance, I decided it was best to have a partner closer to Keith's, erm, abilities. This way we've been able to modify the choreography as we go along. You'll get a better idea of what I mean throughout the session. Law?"

"Yes?" He appeared at her side. While his face had relaxed a little bit, she could feel the tension radiating in his body next to hers. The urge to squeeze his hand and reassure him was almost overpowering; however, Collette was already watching them with far more interest than was purely professional. Best not to give her any wrong impression.

"Why don't we demonstrate what we've worked on from the beginning up to the new part from start to finish, then we can break the new parts down for Keith and Collette?"

"Sure. Let's do this."

They walked to the *X* Fanny had marked on the studio floor with tape so they would know where to begin while staying in the camera's frame. She caught Law's eye and took a deep, exaggerated breath, knowing it would remind him to do the same before pressing Play on the song. They went through the dance from Fanny walking in a circle with Law's admiring gaze never leaving her face all the way to the new lift and the close-frame L-step. They finished with a gentle sway in each other's arms, the slowing of the dance creating an almost hypnotic bubble that felt like no one else in the world existed. The illusion shattered as soon as Collette started cheering and Keith let out a piercing whistle.

Fanny stepped back, pressing the back of her hand against her cheek. Throughout her career, she had performed choreography that was the cardiovascular equivalent of sprinting across a football field, yet she had never felt this warm from the inside out. It was probably the wacky heating system in this old building acting up again, but when she looked back at Law, he seemed as cool as a cucumber. Humph.

"That was amazing, you guys," Collette said enthusiastically. She stood and adjusted the camera on their end, then reached out for Keith's hands. "Come on, darling. Let's see you swing me around like that."

"I'll do my best," he said, bowing slightly.

As usual, Fanny did all the talking through the session, breaking the choreography down step by step. It was easier than she had expected because she found herself often repeating the same corrections for Keith that she had for Law when he first learned the steps. Both men were hampered by a natural stiffness in their hips and a tendency to look down at their feet, which she thought might be a hockey player thing. When cued to look at their partner, however, it was curious that both men had almost the same expression on their faces. The difference being that Keith was actually head over heels in love with his partner while Law was simply well-rehearsed in making women feel precious.

"Keith, for the lift I've found that if I think of it as a side fake, it feels more natural balancing the weight," Law chimed in after Keith had set Collette down in their first attempt. He covered his mouth with one hand, then cringed at Fanny. "I'm sorry, Fanala. I didn't mean to overstep."

"No need to apologize." Fanny held up her hand. "This is why I want you. Here, I mean. In this role as my partner." Oh no, she was overcompensating and the gleam in Collette's eye meant it had not gone unnoticed.

"Fanala?" Collette raised her eyebrows suggestively. "That's a cute nickname."

Fanny shook her head and made a *psssht* noise. "Law keeps trying to guess what Fanny is short for and don't you tell him." She threw a wicked grin in his direction. "He's never going to guess and the torment will eat away at him forever."

"You guys are too cute," Collette said. "You remind me of when Keith and I first got together and I told him I would never date a professional athlete. He wore me down, though," she added, casting an adoring look at her fiancé.

"It's awesome that you're a hockey player, too." Keith nodded at Law. "Thinking about the lift as a side fake really helps. If you're ever in Toronto, let me know and we'll hit the rink together."

Law grinned, shifting his weight from side to side. "That'd be great, man. Same if you're ever playing anywhere in Upstate New York. Crystal Hill isn't that far from Lake Placid."

Collette hooked a thumb at Keith and rolled her eyes. "Fanny, I think our men are forming a bromance in front of our eyes."

The last thing she needed was for the wedding planner to think she had used this job as an excuse to spend time with some admittedly gorgeous guy she liked. "He's not my man. He's just my partner. Now why don't you guys try that lift again?"

Law's phone started to beep from out in the hallway. "Shoot, that's my handyman notification," he said under his breath. "Do you mind if I check real quick? I won't leave if you need me."

"Actually, I must be signing off anyway." Murray spoke for the first time since they had started their session. "Collette and Keith, I'll need a list of who hasn't RSVP'd so I can let the B-list guests know there are openings. Empty tables don't look good in magazine photos. Thank you for your time, Miss Cunningham,

Mr. Carl." His face remained impassive as his screen went black.

Fanny frowned. It hadn't seemed like the wedding planner had been impressed with their coaching skills. The dance had been one of the best they had done, too. If that hadn't been enough for her to get the paycheck she needed, nothing would.

"We've gotta run, too," Collette said. "It's almost eleven o'clock here in London and I've got an early call time on set tomorrow. Keith is here until tomorrow, so we'll work on the new part in my trailer. I really love what you guys have put together for us so far."

"At least somebody does," Fanny said with a sigh as she waved goodbye to the screen before closing the laptop with a slam.

Law took his phone and checked the message, then slid his eyes up to meet Fanny's. "The wedding planner guy's a tough nut to crack, huh?"

She rubbed her forehead wearily. "I don't think the Nutcracker Prince himself could get him to smile," she said, wishing it was Christmas and that a sack of money would appear in her stocking. "Law, if he fires us and goes with someone else, I won't get the commission. What am I going to do?"

"I should have turned my phone off." He

slipped it back into his pants pocket. "But you're not the only one in dire financial straits. I just got the bill for my sewer permit and it's insane. That's not your problem, though," Law said as he shook his head.

A few weeks ago, she would have snapped at him for the interruption. Now, though, she was starting to see things a little differently, rethink snap judgments she tended to make about people. Law wasn't perfect, but he wasn't her old partner either. "You're giving up your time to do this for me and not getting paid a cent. Don't apologize for taking care of yourself, okay?"

Law's eyes widened as if her words had struck a nerve. "Huh." He leaned back against the wall, his eyes drifting somewhere else. "No one has ever said that to me before."

"Law?"

His eyes focused back on hers and he pushed off the wall, starting toward her. "Yes?"

"Don't you have a handyman job to do?"

"Oh, shoot." He turned—with improved co-ordination, Fanny noted with some pride—and ran out the door. "See you next week!" he yelled from the stairway.

She chuckled to herself as she took the ring light down from the barre. When she turned around to face the mirror, the goofy smile on her face was still there. It changed her whole face, lightening the harsh angles of her high cheekbones and making her eyes softer. She looked…happy. It had been a long time since she had seen that in her reflection, felt the thrill radiating throughout her being and coming out of her lips in a soft hum of the song they had just danced to. She did a little twirl and kicked her leg out to the side, higher than she should have. Her hamstrings tightened in response as her hip started to burn.

Clutching the side of her leg, Fanny limped over to the laptop and unplugged it. What had she been thinking, messing around like that? She couldn't dance like that anymore. She wasn't a dancer, and apparently she wasn't all that great a coach or teacher either if the wedding planner's reaction was any gauge. She looked up in the mirror once again.

This time, it felt like she was looking at a stranger.

Without dance, who was she anymore? Until she found the answer for herself, she had no business getting involved with anyone else's life. Not even someone who made her so happy that she danced.

CHAPTER THIRTEEN

LAW HAD BEEN to a lot of different kinds of parties over the years: birthday, engagement, congrats on the removal of your tattoo featuring your ex's name, etc.

But this was his first baby shower.

He tugged on the drawstrings of his hoodie, grateful at least that he didn't have to dress up for this particular festivity. Wearing the button-down shirt, dress pants and those shiny shoes that were the death of comfort for the Zoom call a week ago had been sheer torture. It had served its purpose, though, when Fanny's face had lit up like a spotlight had shone on it. Oh, sure, she had rearranged her expression almost instantaneously, but he had studied her features enough times by now to watch for the subtle signs that he had pleased her. Things only he might recognize, like the way her eyes lightened to a peridot green or the way she bit her full lower lip when she tried to hide a smile.

Looking around the driveway full of cars, he didn't see her little red Honda anywhere. She said she would show up, and when Fanny said something, she meant it. Seeing the table on the porch with the gifts piled on top jogged his memory about the gift card sitting in the passenger seat of his Jeep, so he turned around and walked back to retrieve it, just as the flash of red he had been searching for slowed at the open gate at the entrance to the farm. After she parked and got out of the car, he grinned and nodded to the barn on his left while he waited for her.

"Of all the barns in all the world, you had to walk into mine," he misquoted. "That was a terrible pun. *Casablanca* is my mom's favorite movie, mainly because she always said my dad reminded her of Humphrey Bogart."

"It's actually one of my favorites, too," she confessed as she strolled over to him. "A few years ago, I was in a musical version of it in a small theater in New Jersey. I was so bummed when it didn't make it to Broadway."

"Don't tell my mom that or she'll start an online petition to bring it back," he joked, then held up his present. "What did you get the expectant mama?"

She pulled an envelope out of her large red

purse. "Since I don't know BeeBee or Bill, I figured a gift card from Mama Renata's would be good. From what I've heard, takeout is a godsend when you're a sleep-deprived parent of a newborn."

"It absolutely is." Law nodded, then clarified quickly as both her eyebrows shot up in surprise. "Not that I know from personal experience. But my brother and his wife just had a baby a little over a year ago and they definitely would have appreciated a gift certificate from any of the restaurants in town."

"You and your family seem to be really close," she said, kicking up the dirt as they leaned on the fence in front of the barn.

"We are," he replied. "At least we are now. I wandered for a long time trying to find myself through all these different careers and hobbies and places. When I came back to town to help my folks get their place ready to sell, I finally realized that none of those things defined me. It's the people here, my family, my friends—they're the ones who shaped me. Crystal Hill has always been the one constant in my life. Now it's my turn to make my own mark on it, you know?"

"Mmm," she murmured quietly. "Spoken like a true woodworker."

His right hand twitched and he almost dropped the present he was holding with it. "Just another hobby I gave up on," he said. It was what he told everyone in town when they asked why he had stopped doing woodworking. Easier for everyone to think of him as the same old distractable Lawson rather than have them look at him with pity. Looking past the barn and out over the grazing fields, he added, "c'mon, let's get inside before all of Bill's risotto gets eaten."

Climbing up the steps to the front porch, she rapped the top of the box with her knuckles. "What's in here? A tiny bib that says 'Got milk?'"

He narrowed his eyes at her. "You really don't know me at all, do you SteFANNY?" Law put extra emphasis on the last two syllables of what clearly wasn't her name, by the withering look she gave him. "Now, fair warning. These Crystal Hill gatherings can be a little bit intimidating for newcomers. It's a close-knit community that's not easy to break into overnight. Pretty much the whole town shows up to these things and with all the local gossip and inside jokes, you might feel a little isolated." Setting his gift down on the table, he knocked on the door, then jabbed a thumb at his chest. "Stick with me as your sherpa and I promise you won't be a wallflower for very long."

BeeBee flung the door open, a wide smile on her face. "Hey, you two," she said, grabbing Law in a quick hug then giving Fanny a firm squeeze on the shoulder. "Come on in. It's a full house and there's already a line for the appetizers on the kitchen table. Don't worry, though," she said over her shoulder as she turned and led them through the door. "We'll be moving the party outside into the front yard as soon as Bill and my dad get the tent set up."

They made their way into the great room, which—while normally open and spacious with its bay windows and stone fireplace—was now teaming with people. A low hum of chatter filled the air, along with the delicious smells of fresh bread and herbs. Law put a protective hand on Fanny's lower back to let her know that he would be right there with her in case she felt like a lonely outsider.

"Miss Fanny!" A chorus of high-pitched squeals rang out as several of the girls Law recognized from Fanny's dance class sprinted to her and wrapped themselves around her legs. He quickly found himself shunted to the side by not only the little girls, but their moms.

"I'm so happy to see you," one of the moms

said, handing Fanny a cup of lavender-infused lemonade. "Amaya has been talking nonstop about your class. She was thinking about quitting dance before this year, but since you started, she looks forward to it all week long. I've been trying to find time at the studio to let you know how much of an impact you've made."

"Emily, too," another of the moms chimed in. She pulled her daughter off Fanny's leg while giving Fanny's plum-hued, off-the-shoulder top an appreciative eye. "That is a gorgeous shirt, by the way. You always look so stylish. Someday we should all get together for coffee and you can tell us moms where you find your clothes."

"Come to the bakery and the coffee is on the house," Law's cousin Georgia said. "Oh, hi there, Law," she said, practically elbowing him out of the way to stand at Fanny's side. "We've all been talking about how our kids practically worship you. We were thinking about starting a dance moms book club and we'd love for you to give us some recommendations."

"Well, I'd give a lot more than fashion tips and book recommendations for Georgia's eclairs, so I'm in," Fanny replied, to which the women encircling her broke out in laughter. They pulled her away to the buffet table with so many of the little girls following behind them, she might as well have been Taylor Swift throwing candy at a parade.

"I—I'm right here if you need me," he called after her futilely, as the noise drowned his voice out entirely. Far from feeling abandoned, however, Law smiled at the sight. If she thought the town would embrace her as one of their own, it might end up being a self-fulfilling prophecy. He didn't believe in signs, but if he did, this was a good one, right?

Law rose up on his toes to see if he could spot Lucas and Chrysta. So far, there was no sign of them, so he took a paper plate off the stack on the counter and made his way toward the food. They had pulled out the extra leaf of the kitchen table and it groaned with the trays of garlicky antipasto and crusty bruschetta topped with fresh mozzarella, as well as more typical American fare like pigs in blankets and new potato salad studded with bright green chives. His mouth watered, yet before he could fill up his plate, a commotion over by the living room drew his attention. The children had spotted the table of presents from the window and from the panicked looks on their moms' faces, were preparing to go rogue and storm the battlements.

Before bedlam erupted, Fanny clapped her hands so loudly that the children, even the little boys, froze in their tracks. Walking serenely between the clusters of sticky jam hands and lemonade-stained dresses, she sat on the window seat, effectively blocking their view of the presents table.

"Story time," she said in the musical teacher voice she could switch on like a setting on the remote control. "If everyone can sit crisscross applesauce, Handyman Lawson and I will tell you a story. It's a good one too, so let's put our fingers on our lips to remind us it's listening time." She demonstrated the motion with her long index finger resting on her bottom lip and Law had to swallow hard as he walked over and sat on the seat beside her.

"Erm, what story are we telling?" he muttered out of one side of his mouth as he leaned against her.

"We're improvising, work with me here," she muttered back through a gritted-teeth smile. "This story is called The Fairy Princess and the, erm, Donkey Prince."

"I don't like where this is going," he whispered before putting his hands on his head like donkey ears and letting out a loud bray. "Hee-haw, Your Highness."

Out of the corner of his eye, he saw BeeBee

clap one hand over her mouth and the other over her belly as she shook with laughter.

"Once upon a time," Fanny began, "the graceful fairy princess came to visit the Kingdom of the, uh, Diamond Mountains. She was there to give a magic show for all the boys and girls of the land. Before she could begin, a handsome prince rode up on a white stallion. He promised her all the diamonds in his kingdom if she would agree to be his princess, and as proof of his riches, handed her a beautiful pink diamond bigger than any she had ever seen."

Thinking fast, Law grabbed a peach out of the bowl of fruit on the counter and kneeled in front of Fanny. "A token of my faithful and abiding devotion," he said, attempting his best charming voice that cracked embarrassingly midsentence. It had been a while since he'd tried to charm anyone. Guess he was a little rusty. "Will you save your magic for me and only me?"

"But what the prince didn't know was that one of the fairy princess's powers was to always know when someone was not telling the truth," Fanny went on as she took the peach in one hand before tossing it over her shoulder and into the trash can beside the window seat. "You see, she knew that the diamond was not real. It was only made of cheap glass that the prince gave away to all the pretty princesses while he kept his real treasure hidden away from sight. The fairy princess stood tall and spun in a circle around and around." She stood and motioned for the kids to back away before rising on her toes and twirling with her arms over her head. Coming to a stop when she faced Law, whose knee was starting to protest the kneel, she pointed at him. "With a wave of her wand, the prince and his steed merged into one, a beast with a scraggly tail, thick, ungainly hooves and the largest, most ridiculously pointed ears. He was no longer a prince and the mount no longer a stallion, but a humble donkey with only the prince's handsome face remaining beneath the giant ears."

Fanny bit her lip and looked down at him pointedly. Oh, she was enjoying this and as humiliating as it was, he would do anything to make her happy. Kneeling on all fours with his hands on the ground, he brayed once more as if in anguish. "Hee-hawwww. Man, my handsome, princely figure is ruined! How will I ever find a princess to love me when I have—hee-hawwww—hooves?" He held up his hands in gnarled fists and put them over his face, pretending to weep.

The children laughed uproariously before

Fanny once again put her finger to her lips and they quieted. Forget fairy tales, she really was magic.

"Many years passed and the donkey prince traveled far and wide in search of a cure," she went on, lowering herself back to her seat. "But there was nothing anywhere that could give him what he needed. Finally, he returned home and resigned himself to his fate. He used his sturdy hooves to haul carts up from the mines and till the fields of the farmers, giving back what he could to the people from whom he had hidden his riches for so long."

Law found Caroline among the children and whispered in her ear.

Her eyes lit up and she climbed on his back. Still on his hands and knees, Law paraded his little cousin in a circle around the coffee table, braying happily the whole time.

"At last the fair princess returned and when she saw that he had truly learned his lesson, she returned him to his original form," Fanny said, standing and spinning once more, but in the opposite direction this time.

Law stood up and spread his fingers in front of his face as if amazed by the sight of them. Suddenly, he was hit by the memory of waking up in the hospital after his injury. On the ambulance ride there, the EMTs had prepared him that with a crush injury that severe, there was a very good chance they might need to amputate his arm. He had gone into surgery knowing he might come out of it forever altered, and when he saw all of his fingers sticking out of the plaster cast, it had been like Christmas and his birthday all rolled into one.

"He raced to his treasury, and once there, took out all his diamonds and distributed them to his people, because he had realized that they were his real source of wealth and hope," she continued as Law grabbed a few apples from the fruit basket and juggled them effortlessly in the air, before tossing them to the crowd of children sitting on the floor in front of Fanny. She bubbled up in unrestrained laughter at the sight, unable to control her reaction just this once. "When the fairy princess saw his true heart shining through, she agreed to stay in the kingdom with him and use her magic to help him bring joy and peace to the land. They all lived happily ever after in the kingdom that was now known as the Donkey Kingdom. The end."

The children cheered and began to pull on Law's arms, clamoring for a ride on his back.

BeeBee stepped forward and let out one of her signature ear-piercing whistles. "Kids, wasn't that an awesome story?" Among the shouts of "Yeah!" she called out, "Bill has prepared a pirate-themed obstacle course outside. Last one to get there has to walk the plank into the water buffalo pen." As the kids made a beeline for the door, she held up a hand to the parents. "Don't worry," she said in a loud stage whisper. "We learned our lesson about letting kids play in the water buffalo pen. Bill set up an inflatable ball pit."

While the children were occupied with the elaborate obstacle course BeeBee's husband had set up behind the barn, the adults gathered on the porch to watch BeeBee open presents from the porch swing. After opening onesies, blankets and a pump that looked to Law like a medieval torture device, he tried to appear nonchalant when she pulled open the silver wrapping paper on his gift. He couldn't help stealing a sideways glance at Fanny, though, to make sure she was watching.

BeeBee lifted open the lid to the box and her jaw dropped. His brash cousin whom he had only seen cry when she laughed too hard over a joke she had made at Lucas's expense, now wiped tears out of her eyes with the back of her sleeve.

"What is it?" Georgia asked, raising her chin to try to peek.

BeeBee lifted the present out of the box. It was a panel of wood, a gleaming strip of maple that Law had taken from the woods on his property and hewn down to a foot-long rectangle. Onto its surface, he had carved the image of the grazing fields in front of them with the barn and BeeBee's cows in the foreground and the hills and mountains rising along the edges. He had etched an image of a pregnant BeeBee standing next to Bill in the fields, gazing up at him while her beloved water buffaloes flanked them on either side.

"It's perfect," BeeBee said, her words choked. She stood and held out her arms for him to embrace her in a warm hug. "You even got Fernando's crooked horn and adorable expression just right. This is going to go right over the baby's crib so it's the first thing he or she sees in the morning. Thank you so much, cuz."

He patted her on the back before letting her go. "You're welcome, cuz," he said, shuffling his feet and trying not to cry himself. Stepping back into the crowd, he sought Fanny's eyes for her reaction.

"Oh, Law," she murmured. She looked over at him, blinking away the emotion in her eyes before he could read exactly what that emotion was.

After all the gifts had been opened, the crowd spread out over the farm, with the parents keeping watchful eyes on the kids as they fed fistfuls of hay to the cows, and the single adults clustering around the grill where Chef Bill had a continuous rotation of sizzling burgers, sausages and roasted spring vegetables glazed with a sweet-and-spicy honey marinade. Law wolfed down a sausage before finally tracking Fanny down away from the crowd in the field past the barn.

"Hey, there!" He jogged up to her. "Did you get anything to eat? I can run back and make you a plate. Bill's about to put venison medallions on there and he makes a chimichurri to top them that is out of this world."

"Maybe in a little while," she said, not taking her eyes off the horizon ahead. "What a beautiful view."

"Yes, it certainly is," he said quietly, looking not at the rustling trees or the gentle sloping hills or the guardian mountains in the distance, but at the way her eyes reflected the bright stretch of sweet grass and the way even her wavy dark ponytail danced at the base of her neck.

She turned her head and a corner of her lips

turned up as if she knew what he meant by that. "Can we see your house from here? When it's built, I mean?"

Leaning in toward her, he brushed her arm as he pointed at a valley dipping between the hills. "It will be right there, directly in front of where the sun rises in the morning," he said softly, relishing the floral scent that wafted up from her skin. Even here in the meadow of wildflowers, she smelled like the epitome of spring. "Of course, who knows when that will be." He shrugged and slid his hands in his pockets. "I had to cut the design back again to make room in my budget to hire my contracting crew. I guess a second bathroom was superfluous for just me, right?"

She chuckled, then let out a contented sigh and wrapped her arms around her waist. "It looks exactly like your carving." Fanny shook her head and pivoted to face him. "I thought you said you couldn't do woodworking anymore because of your injury."

He took his right hand out of his pocket and flexed it in front of him. "I can still carve," he said, frowning down at his hand as if he could will it to magically heal. "But it takes twice as long as it used to and after a project like that, I'm living on Ibuprofen for weeks afterward."

"You never act like it bothers you while we're dancing," she said. "Except for that one-handed lift we tried, I never would have known."

"I didn't want you to find another partner," he admitted. "Besides, it's not a big deal. I'm used to powering through. You've probably danced through a lot worse." He slipped his hand back in his pocket and looked back at the farmhouse behind them as peals of laughter rang out from the porch. "I knew BeeBee would love it. Sometimes you make sacrifices for the people you care about."

"Hmm," she said, meeting his eye with the piercing stare that always made him feel like she could strip away the layers of varnish in his glib, one-off remarks. "Still. You're not just some hobbyist, Law. You're an artist. I really hope you can afford rehab or treatment for your injury that will let you get back to your craft someday. It's clear you love it."

"Well." He kicked over a clod of dirt with the toe of his boot "I guess we'll see how the contracting thing works out. So—" he changed the subject and arched an eyebrow at her "—you seemed to do just fine with the usually picky Crystal Hill in-crowd. In a town that's run by its women, winning over the moms is basically a coup." Law's heartbeat picked up the pace as he tried to keep his voice casual. "Ever think about staying here after the recital is over?"

"And do what exactly?"

"Teach dance?" he suggested. "Clearly, the kids in your classes love you." *It's impossible not to*, he thought to himself.

She shook her head, her lips pressing into a single, forbidding line. "You can't make a living just teaching," Fanny said. "Owning a studio is the only way to actually make enough money, and aside from not wanting to compete with my mentor, I would never be able to rival an institution like the one Madame Rousseau has built here. A lot of those moms were students of hers decades ago who are now bringing their daughters for dance classes."

She stopped talking, but Law got the sense there was more she wanted to say. "Is there anything else holding you back?"

"I mean—" she inhaled sharply, then dropped her shoulders and shot him a look that said *Tread carefully* "—ending my dance career feels in some ways like a sudden death. The grief is still fresh and I just feel like I need to start over instead of trying to carry on in the same world. It...it hurts too much to think about what I've lost."

"So why are you teaching at the studio and

choreographing a wedding dance?" Law knew he was pushing the conversation farther than he should. It was a risk he couldn't pass up. He needed to know if there was a chance she might stay here. With him. "You've still got a foot in the world and it doesn't seem like dance is out of your system just yet."

She let out a slow, ragged breath. "The only reason I'm doing those things is because I owe it to the people who asked me," she said. The smile she gave him was sharp and tinged with bitterness. "Sometimes you make sacrifices for the people you care about, right?"

Putting his hands on his hips, Law faced her as she echoed his words back to him. Instead of issuing one of his usual bantering shots, however, he closed his mouth. In the stillness, an understanding deepened in him. They were so much alike, in the ways that really mattered. Fanny's loyalty to her people, her drive to excel at whatever she attempted, the way she thrived when she was part of a like-minded community, whether in the world of dance or with the women and young girls of Crystal Hill. The lens through which they viewed the world was so similar despite the stark contrasts of their passions. Something about the way her face changed, softened, as she looked back at him, gave him hope she realized it, too.

But then, she took a step back, away from him. Taking her phone out of her pocket, she held it up as if using it as a shield against him. "I've really got to get going. I have my call with the life coach in half an hour and I've rescheduled on her twice already."

"Oh, okay," Law said as he gestured toward the driveway. "Let's get you back, then."

She tucked her chin down in a nod and started back in the direction of the cars. As Law followed half a step behind her, she gave a quick turn of her head and caught his eye. "We're still on for practicing the dance Wednesday and Thursday, and the Zoom session with Keith and Collette on Friday, right?"

"Of course," he said. Nearly tripping over a large rock in his path, he caught his balance and wove around it before jogging to reach her side. "Why wouldn't we be?"

"It's just that I was chatting with your brother while we were in line for dessert," she said, taking out her keys and fiddling with them when she reached her car. "He said you're on track to have your license approved soon and that means you can start reaching out to developers and local builders for work. Remember, I'm going to be gone as soon as the recital is done. You shouldn't neglect your own goals just to help me. Anyway," she added, opening the driver's-side door, "this should be the last week I'll need you. We're almost done with the dance. I've been working on a special twist on your 'Hollywood dip.'"

She smiled and gave him a genial wave as she ducked into her car and drove off, but Law was left with a heaviness in his chest that her lighthearted farewell didn't relieve at all.

In no uncertain terms, she had basically told him that she wasn't one of the people he should care enough for to sacrifice his time.

Unfortunately, the sentiment was too little, too late.

He already cared about her more than he had ever thought possible.

CHAPTER FOURTEEN

FANNY RACED UP the stairs of the dance studio and into her apartment like someone was chasing her despite the fact that she had plenty of time before her call.

The afternoon at the baby shower had made two things very clear. The first was that Law had definitely changed from the self-centered, fickle guy she had met ten years ago into a man who cared enough about others to humiliate himself in front of a pack of feral children. He was the kind of guy who would put himself through physical pain just to make a beautiful carving for his cousin's baby. The kind of guy who would take time out of growing his own business to practice a first wedding dance for which he was receiving no compensation at all. He was a guy whom she had wanted to kiss so badly back in the fragrant meadow of wildflowers that she had needed to escape to her car and flee the scene like some sort of romance criminal.

And that led to the second thing she had realized, which was that her next passion needed to get her as far away from him as possible because this time she wasn't the one in danger of getting hurt. It wasn't fair to Law to give him any hope of there being a future between them. Until she knew who she was again, it wasn't right to encourage any of this romantic nonsense. Thank goodness, the life coach would be calling her in a few minutes to set her on the path to her next role in life.

Hopefully a role that took her to Abu Dhabi or Tasmania or Alaska, somewhere far enough away that driving into her car and leaping into Law's waiting arms wouldn't be an option.

Sitting on the small bed, Fanny took a deep breath. She placed a hand on her abdomen in hopes of finding her center. When she danced, it had been a way to engage her core and help her body find its equilibrium for multiple turns balanced precariously on one foot. Now she needed that balance more than ever; this time it was equilibrium between her heart and her head that she sought. Leaving Crystal Hill was the right thing to do for everyone. It was the mature, responsible way to ensure that neither she nor Law ended up any more broken than they already were.

Her phone rang and she checked to make sure it was the life coach before answering.

"Hi, this is Fanny Cunningham," she said with a brightness the life coach would instantly recognize as false. "Are you Desiree?"

A serene voice answered back. "Yes, this is she. Hello, Fanny. It's wonderful to finally get to speak with you."

"I'm so sorry I've had to reschedule this call so many times." Fanny looked down, shaking her head. "Life has been crazy lately, which being a life coach, you probably hear a lot. If things weren't crazy, I wouldn't need a coach, right?"

"I don't like to use the word 'crazy,'" Desiree replied, her tone completely unchanged. "But I understand the sentiment. When we lose direction in life, it can make things feel chaotic. That's where I come in. So I've received your answers to the questionnaire I had you fill out, but why don't you tell me in your own words the questions you have that need answering?"

"Um, well..." Fanny rose from the bed and pointed the toes of one foot in front of her. She had never been able to talk on the phone without dancing, although in this small room that could create more problems than it solved. "See, I am—I was a dancer, all my life. But since my injury, I can't perform professionally in the style of dance I trained in all that time. So now I'm looking for a completely new direction for my career. I'm the type of person who needs more than just a nine-to-five job. I need a passion. We only get this one life, right?" She slid her foot back and rose onto the balls of both feet, lifting the arm that wasn't holding the phone over her head.

"I couldn't agree more," Desiree said. "So, let's see what we have here from your information. You are looking for a pursuit that involves creativity and collaboration with other people."

"Exactly," Fanny said. It had been one of her favorite things about being an ensemble dancer, whether in the ballet company or the chorus line of a musical. They had been a team, working together toward the goal of creating a transcendent experience for the audience. Sure, the soloist roles had been amazing and not a small boost to the ego, but she had found working with the entire cast equally satisfying. "I'm definitely an extrovert. Too much time alone is not good for me."

"Uh-huh. And you are looking for a dynamic field, something with challenges that change from year to year as opposed to a more routine type of operation?"

"I think so." Fanny picked one foot off the ground and tried to balance like a flamingo, lowering her supporting heel to the floor. "I'm not opposed to some routine. Having a set schedule where I know what I'm doing week to week is nice. It's more that I like some variety within the job. I don't like to be bored," she specified. The routine of dance classes every week was something she enjoyed, but rotating to different roles within a show as a swing had kept things from getting stale.

"And you marked as being high importance to be in a leadership position," Desiree said. "Meaning you would prefer to be your own boss as opposed to working for someone else, does that sound correct?"

"Yes." Control freak was perhaps a strong term, but Fanny knew herself well enough to know that working under someone's thumb without having control over her own fate would drive her to distraction.

"All right." Desiree sighed. "Now what I will say is that you have some limitations in terms of your background and work experience being rather…singular."

"Well, that's what's required to become a

professional dancer." Fanny put both feet on the ground now and switched from dancing to pacing. "You have to live, eat, breathe dance. I know I don't have a college degree, but I have over ten years of practical experience."

"Yes, but all in the same field," Desiree pointed out. "To completely change course at this stage would require retraining. It doesn't have to be a college degree per se. However, most positions that might meet some of your requirements, such as cosmetology or culinary arts, would require at the bare minimum a certification."

Fanny wrinkled her nose. She had done enough stage makeup and hair over the years to know cosmetology wouldn't be something she enjoyed, and cooking wasn't far behind. "I don't mind working hard. Although, neither of those things really strike me as the best fit. Ideally, it would be nice to find something I can get started in as soon as possible. And I don't mind relocating, just so we're clear. I toured all over the place as a professional dancer, so I'm used to living out of a suitcase."

Far, far away from Crystal Hill and Lawson and his crinkly-eyed smile.

Desiree cleared her throat. "Fanny, as a life coach, I try to be as honest with my clients as possible," she said. For the first time, the woman's voice sounded slightly stern. "Judging from your answers on the questionnaire and from our conversation, something tells me that you're not really ready to move on from dance. Even if you can't perform professionally the same way you are used to, isn't there some way you can continue in this passion you've cultivated over years of hard work simply in a different capacity? Can't you use your experience to contribute to the next generation of dancers who would surely benefit?"

"Basically, those who can't do, teach?" Fanny let her head fall back as she stared desperately at the ceiling fan. "But you see, that's the problem. I don't want to teach dance. I mean, I like teaching and, frankly, I'm great at it. It's just that…teaching feels like a step backward. Like admitting I'm a failure." As soon as Fanny said the words out loud, she realized how true they were. In her mind, she had always viewed people who taught dance as the ones who gave up. She hadn't given up. She had been forced out sooner than she was ready.

"So it's better to run away than admit defeat?" Desiree said gently. "You said your career was ended with an injury. I assume that means it was a sudden end, yes?"

"Yes," Fanny admitted, sinking onto the edge of the bed then sliding onto the floor. "My partner dropped me and I had to have surgery on my hip that limited how high I can lift my leg. The whole reason I switched from ballet to musical theater was to extend my career as long as possible. Instead, it took away years I could have had to prepare myself for a life after performing."

"Aha," Desiree said quietly. "Fanny, it sounds like what you need before you can move on to the next chapter of your life is closure on the last. Now, closure can mean different things to different people. You need to figure out what that means to you, whether it's resolving feelings of anger toward your former partner or finding a way to finish your performing career on your own terms. Then I think you'll be able to see your next steps with greater clarity."

"Hmm," Fanny grunted as she stretched her legs in front of her and flexed her toes, the slight pain of the stretch in her calves a welcome distraction from the groaning pain in her heart. Desiree was right. Fanny was running away, trying to escape the disappointment rather than accept it. She didn't want to leave dance; it was her first and greatest love. Imagining a life without it had been so unthinkable she had needed to hire a life coach to do it for her.

"I know this wasn't what you wanted to hear," Desiree said after a momentary pause. "If you want to take some time and think over what I've said, I'm happy to schedule another call. Does that sound all right to you?"

"I—I think so," Fanny said. "Thank you for your time."

"Of course," Desiree said. "Feel free to reach out by email whenever you're ready. Take as long as you need."

When they hung up, Fanny let her hand holding the phone fall to the floor. Closure. It sounded so simple. But how was she supposed to close the curtain on a stage she would never be able to perform on again? It was impossible.

Sitting on the hardwood floor was starting to make her hip ache. Fanny pushed to a stand, a desperate, clawing need to move and do something forcing her out of the apartment, down the stairs, past the studio and out into Jane Street. She stood there, frozen, as people went about their daily lives in and out of the shops. The trees along the sidewalk had burst into light pink flowers and robins perched merrily on the wrought iron lampposts. It was an idyllic scene, the kind of small-town living so many people dreamed about, yet Fanny didn't know where she fit in among them. She couldn't deny a part of her wanted to stay here with Lawson, to see where these feelings growing deeper each time she saw him might lead. But then who was she? Just another one of his girlfriends, and if he got tired or bored or scared of the commitment and moved on, then who was she? No longer a dancer, no longer the woman he looked at with adoration in his eyes, she would be lost, adrift. Invisible. And for someone who had spent years in the spotlight, that fate was worse than anything else she could possibly imagine.

She turned and headed back up the stairs, and the second she opened the door to the studio, her panic instinctively diminished. Fanny walked along the barre, the feel of the wood under her hand and the familiar smell of the rosin soothing her. This was home, no matter how far she traveled or how badly she tried to deny it.

Desiree had been right. She wasn't ready to give up this world yet.

Fanny left the studio and stood in the lobby. The poster with her and her former partner loomed from the end of the hallway. Normally, she tried to walk past it as quickly as possible. Now she walked toward it, one hand on her still-throbbing hip as she reached out with the other to touch the frame, as if reassuring herself the graceful woman with her leg swept up by her head had once been her. Closure was what Desiree had said she needed to figure out what the next step would be. Maybe the life coach had been right about that, too.

Trudging back up to her room, Fanny reached for her laptop off the bedside table and opened it up. Her former partner had his own website and an email where he could be reached. She had blocked him on all her social media, so she had no idea what he was up to or where he was in the world, but if reaching into the past was the key to her future, then that was what she would do. She was a dancer, now and always, and dancers could do hard, painful things.

But before she could start typing, she noticed a new email in her own inbox from the wedding planner. Her heart caught in her throat. If he was firing her, then none of this mattered, because she wouldn't be able to afford any kind of future, whether in dance or anything else. Putting a hand on her stomach to quell the sickening fear, she opened it.

Dear Miss Cunningham,
This is Murray the wedding planner! I wanted to reach out and first of all apologize for my terse reaction to your demonstration on the Zoom call. You see, I had been interviewing new caterers and I'm afraid that one of them

had served me a salmon mousse that was neither salmon nor moose (ha ha).

I was very impressed by what you've done in such a short period of time, especially given Keith's, shall we say, lack of natural grace. I have seen him and Collette rehearse in person since your last session and I feel quite certain their first dance will be the talk of the town! As the wedding is coming up in just three weeks, I wanted to reach out and let you know that your check will be in the mail as soon as you confirm your mailing address for me. Will you be remaining in Crystal Hill or do you have imminent plans to travel elsewhere? I myself will be on the East Coast soon for a tour of wedding shows and expos over a six-month period as I'm hoping to take my wedding planning bicoastal and set up an office in Manhattan.

Thank you for all your hard work and I look forward to seeing the final result at the wedding. If only all my contractors (especially the caterers) were as efficient and effective as you and your partner, I would be one happy wedding planner!

Best of luck in all your future endeavors,
Murray Fiorino
Fiorino's First-Class Event Planning, Inc.

Fanny read the message several times, in

slight disbelief over both the length and ebullient content of the email from a man who had seemed so taciturn. Although a bout of food poisoning would turn anyone irritable, she knew, having eaten more than her share of hotel-room-service chicken past its prime during her own days on tour.

Suddenly an idea clicked, a confluence of opportunity and timing that seemed practically fated even though she didn't believe in such a thing. She bit her lower lip, yet couldn't hold back the widening smile, as a possible way to have everything she wanted came tantalizingly into view.

CHAPTER FIFTEEN

When Law first got the quote from the website designer, he almost choked on the grilled brie and blackberry preserves sandwich Chrysta had made for him at the cheese shop. A very large part of him had thought about not having a website at all and just hoping that word of mouth would be enough, but Lucas had convinced him it was necessary, and as irritatingly usual, his younger brother was right.

Within a week of the website going live, he had messages requesting quotes for work, the largest one by far coming from Joe Napolitano. In the message he made it very clear that the sale of the dance studio to Napolitano Fitness was not final and therefore everything was still very much confidential, but that he expected it to go through and wanted a crew ready to get right to work as soon as it did. Even after paying his crew, Law would still net enough of a profit from the job to pay off all the legal bills for the LLC and have sufficient funds left over to start pouring the foundation for his house. It would mean financial security, the first stepping stone to his future.

It would also mean the end to any chance of that future being with Fanny.

But as he walked up the stairs to the dance studio for their last week of rehearsals and recording sessions before the big wedding, Law reminded himself that she had only mentioned in passing the idea of running a studio *similar* to the one here. Settling for less than perfect was his MO, not hers. As much as it hurt to even think about her leaving forever, he wasn't going to stand in the way of her achieving her passion, and in fact, would do everything he could to make her dreams come true. Even if that meant saying goodbye.

"Law, I'm so happy to see you!" Fanny bounced into the corridor in front of the changing rooms and grabbed him by the shoulders.

So startled by her enthusiasm that he almost fell into a rack of tutus next to the wall, Law brushed away the web of pink tulle and smiled back at her. "I'm happy you're happy, Fanatalia."

"Worst guess yet." She smiled back. "Hurry in. We only have half an hour in this studio today. Madame Rousseau closed the other one off to have someone come in to do some testing of the wall integrity or something, so the intermediate class got moved to this room."

"Huh." Law swallowed. Napolitano was probably having an appraiser test whether or not a wall was load-bearing or not so he knew if he could tear it down. But he couldn't say that to Fanny because it would put him under potential legal risk if he shared what he knew about the pending sale. "Well, no time to waste, then. Let's get dancing."

"First, I have something I need to talk to you about," she said, taking him by the hand and pulling him into the studio.

As usual he followed her lead. Her face was unusually bright and she almost skipped as she dropped his hand and reached into her bag for her phone. Whatever was happening must be good. Law couldn't resist a small chuckle at the way even her ponytail seemed to swing with extra pep as she danced her way back and opened up the screen on her phone to show him.

"So, I got an email from the wedding planner," she went on, scrolling with one finger until she stopped at the one from Murray. "He apparently wasn't feeling well the day we had the Zoom call with him and that's why he looked like one of the statues from Easter Island when he watched us. He's actually very nice and extremely pleased with what we've done for Keith and Collette. So pleased, in fact, that when I had the idea to join him on his tour of wedding shows and expos to demonstrate our 'first dance for nondancers' method, he jumped right on board."

"I'm sorry, what?"

"He wants us to go on tour with him as featured contractors!" she squealed. Law had never heard Fanny squeal before. It was high-pitched and also somehow enchanting. "He said so many guys are intimidated by the idea of learning to do a choreographed dance, but that you being a nondancer who can do these moves is proof of concept. Anyway, he's doing a six-month tour of wedding shows to get publicity for the East Coast branch of his wedding planning business and he's paying us to go along and perform!" She shook her head, her eyes wide with disbelief. "It's the perfect opportunity. I get to stay in the dance world, perform and tour. I thought I would never get to do that again, and sure, I know it's not going to be the same, but it's still better than nothing, right?"

"Six months," he repeated, rolling the words over in his head and letting them break free before their impact truly hit him. "And he wants... both of us?"

He had come to the studio that morning resigned to a future without her in it. Now everything had changed. Sure, six months wasn't a lifetime, but it was six months with her, sharing rides, meals, dancing and holding her close. All of the things he wasn't ready to let go of yet and now there was a chance to extend their time together. And after six months, who knew? Maybe by then she would see how good they were together and give them a real shot to see where their feelings could lead.

"Of course he wants both of us." She shook her head as if it was obvious. "We're a team. I couldn't have done any of this without you. If you want to," she added, her fingers twisting the long skirt attached to her leotard. "I guess I shouldn't have necessarily assumed you didn't have anything...or anyone else keeping you here."

He swallowed hard. She needed his help and he had come through. There was no better feeling and yet it was tinged with guilt over the fact that he couldn't yet tell her why his answer wasn't an immediate, enthusiastic yes. "Can I have some time to think about it? It's not that I don't want to do this with you," he rushed to assure her as her face scrunched in obvious disappointment. "But being away six months is a long time. I need to make sure I could get my ducks in a row before leaving."

"Okay." She nodded. Her eyes fell on the clock above his head and widened with alarm. "Let me know as soon as you can. In the meantime, we need to get moving. There's one final part of the dance I have to teach you before we record it tomorrow. It won't be a Zoom session since Keith and Collette are both busy, but we'll do a video and send it to both of them to practice on their own."

"When is the wedding again?"

"Two and a half weeks," she replied, picking up one foot like a stork to buckle the clasp on her dance shoe. "So we should be able to have at least one more Zoom session with them before that. Then we'll have another week to rehearse the dance before we perform it at the recital."

The dates raced around Law's head too fast for him to keep them all straight. Joe Napolitano had said in his email that he hoped to have Madame Rousseau's approval of the sale by the end of the month. That meant if he didn't go on this tour with Fanny, she would have zero reason to ever come back here again. However, if he left Crystal Hill, the momentum for his business would collapse. The contract with Napolitano was the springboard for the life he had planned here in Crystal Hill with his family. How was he supposed to make this choice?

"Um, Lawson?" Fanny leaned in front of him and waved a hand in front of his face. "You kind of spaced out on me there."

"I'm sorry." He shook his head and held out his arms in the dance frame. "Ready for our first dance?"

She placed her hand in his and gazed up at him with a new emotion shining in her eyes that sent thrills of hope down his spine. "Always."

Law pulled her close, barely able to breathe between the pounding of his heart. They did the dance all the way through the last part she had taught him where they walked together and ended in a sway.

"Now," she said, slightly out of breath from the quickness of the last few steps. "I'm going to pull away from you here, but keep holding on to my arm, slowly releasing until you're just barely grasping onto my fingertips." She demonstrated doing small crossover steps with her feet and pulling her outstretched arm away from him even as he maintained a loose hold on her as long as he could. "Here's where we're going to do a modification on your 'Hollywood dip' suggestion. I twirl into you like this—" she spun toward him, pulling his arm around her waist until they stood side by side with him holding her close, his right arm tucked over hers "—but instead of a straight dip, you're going to lean toward your left with me on your side like a fulcrum."

"Look at you with the handyman terms," he joked, stepping to the side with his left foot and leaning in that direction with his body. "This feels incredibly unstable by the way."

Her entire body weight was pressed against his right side like the invisible force that slowly pushed the Tower of Pisa off its axis. When he turned his head to look at her, her face was close enough that he could brush his nose against hers if he moved it even a hair closer.

"Remember, it's all about sharing the load," she said. "We're perfectly stable as long as you don't try to pull me too much in your direction or vice versa. But we're not going to stay like this long."

That was a good thing because his right hand, which was still clasped around her and holding her to his side, was beginning to spasm and ache with that familiar pain. "What happens next?"

"You're going to release the hold just enough for me to turn to face you." She did the turn in slow motion as he loosened his grip on her, still keeping his right arm circled around her waist. "Then catch me in a dip with your left arm, moving your right hand over my left thigh." Grinning as they stood face-to-face, she continued. "Collette's reception dress has a long slit so this is going to make a perfect shot for the photographer."

Law's first instinct, as usual when it came to her overconfidence about his dance capability, was to protest that this move was far too difficult for him and was she sure she wanted to risk being dropped on her head for a nice photo op. Every time she would goad and tease and challenge him until he tried it and inevitably found that he could actually do it, even if it took a couple of misfires to get it right. It drove him crazy, mainly because she was always right, and also because somehow he loved that she brought out a bravery in him he didn't know he had. So this time, he didn't second-guess himself, or try to get her to settle for an easier path. He simply tried.

Arching her back, she fell slowly against his left arm as he steered his right from her back down to her gracefully extended left leg. It had been so easy, yet as he watched their reflection in the mirror it had looked incredibly impressive, like he actually knew what he was doing.

He turned his head back to look down at her face glowing in triumph. "That was amazing," Law said, fully in awe of what she had made him accomplish.

"It was," she whispered breathlessly. There was no edge of sarcasm in her voice, no roll in her eyes as they searched his face. Not even a hint of "told ya so." As he slowly, gently brought her back to a standing position, she kept her hands on his arms like she still needed him to steady her through the transition. Nothing in the world made him feel stronger than being the one she relied on to hold her; however, at the same time nothing made him feel as vulnerable. If his hand slipped, if she was hurt because of him, Law would never forgive himself.

A momentous shift, like the moving of continents, passed between them as his eyes remained locked on hers before falling to the parting of her full lips. She bent her head toward him and Law brought his face to hers, knowing after this moment nothing in his life would ever be the same. His lips pressed into hers for only a second, yet long enough for electricity to jolt throughout his entire body. It was like being struck by lightning—except the thundering sound ringing in his ears would have come before lightning, wouldn't it? Then he opened his eyes to realize it wasn't thunder, but actual applause coming from the crowd of middle school girls gathered outside the open studio door as they arrived for their intermediate class.

He and Fanny jumped apart and her hand rushed to her lips as her cheeks flooded with pink.

"Girls," she said in her usual "I'm in charge and woe to anyone who gets on my bad side" sharp tone. "I think you're supposed to be stretching out there. Mr. Carl and I are still in rehearsal for the wedding dance. That's all. Nothing more to see here."

They dispersed, leaving trails of giggles in their wake, and Fanny bit her lip, looking down and shaking her head at the same time.

"I guess we got a little carried away." Law put his hands on his hips. "I for one blame Harry Connick Jr."

Fanny lifted her chin and raised an eyebrow at him. "Law, I didn't even put the music on yet."

"Still," he said, taking a step toward her and reaching for her hand. "If you want me to forget that that just happened, I can. I know we're just dance partners and nothing more." He looked down and skated a thumb across the back of her hand before staring deeply into her eyes again. "Right?"

It was a statement she had made before and at the same time a dare to admit she had been wrong about her feelings for him. Law hadn't known Fanny for long, but he knew her well enough to know she couldn't back away from a challenge, even if it was one that she couldn't win.

She opened her mouth, closed it, then the corners of those beautiful lips turned up in the most genuinely sweet smile, almost as if she was surprised by her own joy. "I don't want you to forget it," she said quietly but sincerely, looking up at him with shining eyes. "You're more than just another dance partner to me, Law." She glanced down at their entwined hands. "Maybe on the tour we can, you know, go out to dinner together or something."

"Something," Law echoed as he squeezed her fingers.

A rap sounded on the door and Madame Rousseau tipped her head to one side. "I'm not interrupting rehearsal, am I?"

Fanny turned her head over her shoulder and as her body followed the motion, she let go of Law's hand. "We're just finishing up," she said, swiveling her chin over her shoulder to cast a sideways look back at him. "I'm teaching the intermediate class, aren't I?"

Madame Rousseau nodded, clasping her hands together. The skin above her prominent veins was paper-thin and she had bruises on her forearm that looked like they were from recent blood draws. "Yes, but before you do, I just wanted to let you know that I have received a serious offer for the dance studio and the theater that I am considering taking. Appraisers are coming to look over the space and they're going to be up in the apartment today, that's why I wanted to let you know ahead of time what was going on."

Fanny's head turned sharply and he couldn't see her face at all. However, the muscles in her back, visible in the low dip of her leotard, tightened and her shoulders lifted almost up to her ears. "Madame Rousseau, are you sure this is what you want to do? This place is your legacy." She threw her hands out to the side. "Isn't there anything the town can do to help you keep it going?"

"It's certainly not what I want," Madame Rousseau said with a sharp inhale, following it with a dry, barking cough. "But running this business is an intense job. I just don't have the stamina for it anymore. And I can't ask the town to go out of its way to find someone who wants to run a dance studio if there is a buyer who will bring more revenue to them using it as a gym."

"A gym?" Fanny's words dripped with disdain. "Like one of those awful chains where they give you a free spray tan for every member you recommend? This beautiful, historic theater being turned into a weight room just breaks my heart."

Law fought the urge to rush forward and hold her. It seemed disingenuous given that he was in talks with the man responsible for Fanny's dismay. He cleared his throat and walked next to her. "It's not that bad, right? I mean, a gym could be a good thing and maybe they could use the studio space for, like, Pilates or dance aerobics or something. Besides," he said, trying desperately to make her—and his conscience—feel better, "you're not going to be teaching here in a few months anyway. Who knows what will happen after you get back from the tour?"

She turned to face him with a face so disheartened Law felt like something had just stabbed him in the chest. "I know," she said, gesturing toward Madame Rousseau. "And Madame Rousseau should do whatever is best for her health, obviously. It just makes me so sad to think of the town losing the one space it has dedicated to the performing arts. Every time we sacrifice a theater or a school music program in favor of something that turns a profit, it's like stealing from the next generation. This isn't about me or my future. It's about the future of this town and all the girls and boys whose only exposure to the arts comes from places like this. It's something I care about, and you should, too."

"How are you always right about everything?" Law heaved his shoulders in a sigh, then looked over at Madame Rousseau. "You said you haven't made up your mind yet, though. Is there a chance the sale won't go through?"

"It really depends on whether or not someone else comes forward with enough money to make the renovations necessary to keep the studio and theater going as they are," Madame Rousseau said with her palms turned up to the ceiling. "On top of that, I would need someone to take my place to run it. If we had the money, I could keep going until we find someone who wants to keep it as a dance studio, but I don't have the resources or the energy to do both." She shrugged. "Anyway, I just wanted to let you know. The intermediate class is ready to start now, Fanny dear."

Fanny turned to Law with a dejected droop to her normally elegant posture. "I guess that's that," she said, quirking her mouth up on one side like a sad clown. "You'd better get going before the dancers come in and start singing about us k-i-s-s-ing in a tree. Middle school girls are like honey badgers someone starved for two days then unleashed onto a buffet. They're aggressive and pounce when they sense weakness. There's no hope for me, but you can save yourself."

He touched her on the arm, briefly, but long enough for her to know he cared. "Call me if you need anything, okay?"

She bobbed her head quickly and touched her eyes with one hand. "Thanks. I'll see you tomorrow."

"Tomorrow," he replied, touching his head in a quick salute.

By then maybe he would have come up with a plan to fix the mess he was at least in part responsible for causing. Yet when the sun rose and tomorrow became today, he still had no answers to the questions that had kept him awake all night. He did, however, have handyman errands to run, starting at the dairy farm where BeeBee needed him to install a ceiling fan in her nursery.

As he banged his hammer into the ceiling, BeeBee and Jackie, the oldest Long sister, appeared in the doorway. Jackie winced with each resonant clang, while BeeBee simply raised the already-louder-than-normal volume of her voice to be heard over the clamor.

"The doctor recommended a ceiling fan for good air flow," BeeBee practically yelled even though Jackie was standing right next to her. "I was just going to get one from the hardware store across from the library, but Bill insisted on special ordering this one from Switzerland or somewhere." She shook her head with a loving smile and shouted, "He's so over the top!"

"Over the what?" Jackie said, covering her ears and cringing.

"I'm almost done." Law turned his head over his shoulder and looked down at the women from his stepladder. "One more should do it. There." After checking to make sure the fan would properly rotate, he climbed down and wiped the sweat off his forehead with the back of his left arm as he hooked the hammer back onto his belt with the right. "You should be all set."

"Wow." Jackie walked into the room, gazing from side to side at the decor. "This looks amazing. Law, your friend Sarge did a great job."

"Isn't it beautiful?" BeeBee's face glowed as she leaned one hand on the edge of the tall wooden crib. "I love that he did the whole accent wall in a mural to look like the grazing fields. It's the perfect spot to hang the piece Law carved."

Warmth spread through Law's chest as he ducked his head. Crossing his arms over his chest, he looked from side to side. "I'm glad you're pleased. Sarge has a really great artistic eye. I love the cow-print rug and the little barnyard stencils he painted on the changing table." The room was earthy with browns and greens interspersed with little pops of light blue in the pillows on the rocking chair in the corner and the lamp on top of the dresser. He had even used local slate for the floating shelves on which BeeBee had placed all the board books she had gotten at her shower. It was cozy and homey without being overly cute. He was definitely hiring Sarge to decorate his house when he was ready for that stage. Of course, going on tour with Fanny would be pushing his house building so far into the distance it was starting to seem like a miniature version of the life he wanted someday. If he left for six months, would it disappear altogether?

"These colors will be great for a boy or a

girl," Jackie said, picking a book off the shelf and flipping through it. "Of course, either way, we'll have another generation of dairy farmers to take care of the herds."

"If they want to," BeeBee said, rubbing her belly. "Or maybe they'll inherit Bill's cooking abilities. Goodness knows they won't learn anything in the kitchen from me. Maybe they'll be a dancer like their Aunt Lou. Chrysta said they're starting Bell in the Mommy and Me ballet class next year. It would be so fun to watch the kids do recitals together or go digging with the Junior Rockhounds club Georgia's boyfriend started at the school." She jutted her chin in Law's direction. "Remember how we used to play in the woods and you would build all us girl cousins tiny fairy houses out of the little bits of wood and moss we found?"

"I'm amazed you remember that," he said, slipping his hands in his pockets. "You couldn't have been more than five or six." Law chuckled and shook his head. "We'd stay outside for hours in the summertime. If Lucas hadn't brought little bags of cheese and crackers for everyone, we would have starved."

"You know, I think most of my best childhood memories revolve around you and me and Jackie and Lucas hanging out together," Bee-

Bee said. She grimaced and clapped a hand on his shoulder. "We probably drove you crazy following you guys around like little puppy dogs. Sorry about that."

"You really didn't," Law assured her. "Lucas was always so serious, even as a kid. If it weren't for you guys, I would never have had any fun. It was like having my own little gang of outlaws, ready for adventure. I think that's the best way to grow up, having lots of family close in age. That's what I want when I have kids."

The happiness of his past merged with his ideas of a future that he now wanted with a surprising urgency. Being the "fun uncle" was fine and all, but being in this room, watching his cousin anchor her roots deeper into their hometown, made the restless stirring in his heart cry out for the same peace. Family. Home. Love. These weren't just abstract concepts anymore. They were everything and he wasn't going to settle for less.

"You'd better hurry up, then," Jackie admonished him. She set the book carefully back on the shelf and wagged a finger. "Bell's a year and a half and BeeBee's due in October." She sighed. "At least you've got Fanny. Given the small percentage of available men in this town, the odds of me finding a guy to marry and have kids with are worse than being struck by lightning."

"Fanny and I are..." Law trailed off. What were he and Fanny? She had admitted they were more than dance partners. That could mean a lot of things. Romantic partners, business partners, partners in crime. All of the above sounded appealing as long as he was with her. He loved how she made him feel like he could do anything, and if he doubted it, she narrowed her eyes with that determined expression and made it her mission to prove him wrong. With her, nothing seemed impossible and everything was a lot more fun, from dancing to telling stories to a gaggle of wild children. She made him better and he was pretty sure she would do the same for the town if he could only convince her to stay. The only problem was the one thing she cared about enough in Crystal Hill—the dance studio—was going to go away if he didn't do something to stop the sale. "I gotta go make some phone calls."

He stayed on the phone through late into the evening and into the next morning. By the afternoon, when he headed back to the dance studio for his final recording session with Fanny, he had some of the answers to some of his problems.

The rest depended on her.

Law hadn't been so equally terrified and excited to see her again since the first time they had danced together. He was, once and for all, going to be able to tell her everything. Everything that had happened since they met, everything he felt for her and everything he hoped for in the future. There was a very good chance she would shoot him down. It was a risk he was willing to take. Heck, it was a risk he had to take because the alternative was watching her leave for good.

Opening the door to the studio, he gave her his most charming smile, the one he usually had to think of panda bears and ice cream to gin up, yet today, for her there were no pandas required.

"Hi, there, Fanalenda," he greeted her in typical Rumpelstiltskin style. "Are you ready for our last first dance?"

She stood up from crouching over the laptop set up on the folding chair with her back to him. In the mirror, her reflection did not return his smile. "Let's get this done," she said quickly.

He scratched his chin. Something wasn't right here, but living with the women of Crystal Hill had taught him that sometimes it was better not to ask them what was wrong because then they would have to tell you what was wrong and that only added another unnecessary task to their endless list. It was very likely she was simply stressed about getting the dance right for their last session, in which case the best thing to do was to follow her instructions and "get this done."

However, as soon as he hit his mark on the studio floor and she flipped on the music, Law could tell something else was definitely bothering her. She didn't smile or pretend to be in love with him. She barely looked at him unless the choreography called for it and when they went into the "Hollywood dip" her back was so tense and stiff, he almost lost his grip on her because he expected her back to arch meltingly like it did before.

As the music faded, she brusquely stood upright and slammed the laptop closed. Grabbing her dance bag and heaving it over her shoulder, she marched out of the dance studio without looking back.

Law had to run to catch up with her on the sidewalk in front of Big Joe's. "Fanny, what's happening?"

At last she looked at him, her eyes ablaze with green fire. "What's happening is that I'm hungry and I'm going to get a milkshake. Is that all right with you?" Shoving the door open, she stormed inside the diner, not bothering to wait for him to respond.

If there was one thing Law had experience with, it was women being mad at something he did. Whatever this was about, he was obviously to blame.

Following her inside, he tried to ignore the heads swiveling in their booths as he walked up to the counter to stand next to her. "Look, I don't understand what's going on here, but it's clear you're mad at me. So I'm going to go ahead and apologize because it certainly wouldn't be the first time I did something stupid that ticked someone close to me off. Or the second."

"Or the third," Joe Kim supplied unhelpfully as he poked his head out from the opening of the kitchen behind the counter.

"Are you apologizing because you're going to say no to the tour even though you made it seem like you were on board, or are you apologizing because the reason you're saying no to the tour is because you're working with Joe Napolitano on demolishing that beautiful dance studio, or are you apologizing for lying to me about the whole thing and making me feel like a fool for trusting you?" Fanny faced him with her arms clenched tight in a knot across her chest and her cheeks even paler than usual. She whipped her head around toward the kitchen. "I'd like a black-and-white milkshake, please, Joe. Extra whipped cream."

"Yes, ma'am," Joe said with uncommon meekness before disappearing back into the kitchen.

"I was going to tell you everything today after we finished our last recording session," Law said, gesturing toward the direction of the dance studio next to the diner. "There's a lot I need to catch you up on. If we can just sit down and talk, I can explain and you might still be mad at me, but at least you'll have all the information."

"Might?" She barked out a mirthless laugh and slammed a $5 bill on the counter. "There's no 'might' about any of this. You covered up your involvement with Joe Napolitano even though you knew how upset I was about the studio being turned into a gym. You gave me hope that I would get a chance to go back on tour with a partner I could actually count on when you had no intention of going anywhere."

"That's not true," Law protested. "I'm not saying no to the whole tour. But six months is a long time, Fanny. I'm still growing a business here, building a house. I thought maybe once we had all the details, we could talk about just being gone for a short time, like a couple of months, instead of six."

"And then what?" she asked as Joe brought a tall goblet with the milkshake and a towering mound of whipped cream to the counter before silently sliding the money toward the cash register. "After two months, you expect me to follow you back here and watch while you tear down the one resource for the arts this town has in favor of some meathead muscle palace?"

"That's what I wanted to tell you," Law said. "I couldn't say anything before because Napolitano asked me to keep the potential sale on the down-low and you had made it very clear you weren't going to stay here a minute longer than necessary after the recital."

"Yeah, well, that's how fast things can change," she said. Her voice was quieter now, still angry, but tinged with a bitterness that caught him off-guard. She was so many things, a kaleidoscope of colors and emotions, yet regretful wasn't something he had gotten from her before. "One minute you're flying in the air, the next you're landing flat on the ground on your hip. I should have known better than to trust you and that's on me." She grabbed the milkshake and pulled it to the edge of the counter, leaning one side against the Formica as if she needed the assist.

"You can trust me. That's what I'm trying to tell you." Law took her milkshake in one hand, her elbow with the other and led her to the booth by the window. Setting the glass down, he motioned for her to sit. She did, stiffly and gracefully as a queen trying to decide whether or not to let him keep his head. "I'm not doing the job with Napolitano. I called him back this morning to let him know that I spoke with the members of the local business association who I've gotten to know very well over the last month or so and they have concerns over the aesthetics of a chain gym in such a prominent downtown spot. I also spoke with the zoning board, and since the process of getting a sewer permit around here is like one of the seven labors of Hercules, I mentioned that people in town would probably be pretty displeased about a business from Bingleyton getting priority of multiple bathrooms and showers for one locker room when they were paying a fortune for a single-family home permit. Napolitano's pulling out of the sale. The dance studio is staying put and I thought, maybe, you would want to stay, too. To run it, that is," he added, flattening his palms on the table to demonstrate that he was laying everything out on the open.

"So you think I should give up my last chance at touring, at ending my career on the road on my terms, to run the studio here in Crystal Hill." She poked at the milkshake with the straw angrily, watching the whipped cream melt into the mixture.

"Hey, I was willing to meet you halfway and go on tour for at least part of the time," Law said defensively. "I feel like you're not being fair here."

"I only asked you for a few months and you balked. This is my entire future we're talking about and I've learned from experience not to sacrifice more of myself than the other person is willing to give. Lawson, I want to go on tour to get closure with the dance world, not because I want to stay in it for the rest of my life. The life coach said that this is the only way I'll be able to move on and find a new passion."

"So you're running away," Law shot back. "Because some yahoo on the internet who doesn't know you said this was the thing to do. I've spent almost every day with you for the past month, Fanny. I know you and I know dance is who you are. Whether you're performing or teaching, you can't run away from it. That's how

I feel about Crystal Hill. I wandered all over the country trying to find myself, and it was the people here, my family, my roots, that make me feel whole. I belong here and I think you do, too, but you're afraid of getting hurt again."

"Oh, that's rich," She jerked her chin up and pointed a finger at him. "You're accusing me of being afraid? You're so afraid of commitment, you can't even stick with a single house plan. Why would I settle down here for someone who's just going to drop me the second something shiny and new comes along? That's what you do, Lawson. You give up on things, on people. On yourself. You have the nerve to talk to me about letting go of dance when you just noped out of woodworking after your injury rather than put in the work of recovery, even though you're as much of an artist as I am." Pushing away her untouched milkshake, she stood and started to head for the door, then dropped her head and twisted around to face him. She bit her lower lip and inhaled deeply before piercing him with hardened eyes. "Unlike you, I can keep a promise. I'll still perform the dance at the recital with you because I promised Madame Rousseau we would do it to try to get more boys in the town interested in dance. But other than tech and dress rehearsals the week of the recital, I don't want to see you or hear anything from you. I'll do the last Zoom session with Collette and Keith on my own, then find someone else to go on tour with. It doesn't have to be you." Shaking her head, she tossed the crumpled napkin in her hand on the table. "You're just another guy who wasn't strong enough to hold on to me."

Just like she had ten years ago, she whirled on her heel and pushed open the door to leave him behind.

CHAPTER SIXTEEN

ONE WEEK LATER, Fanny entered the video call with Collette and Keith, hoping against hope that they wouldn't ask about Law.

Naturally, the first thing Collette said was, "Why are you by yourself? Where's the hunky handyman?"

Fanny's head dropped while Keith's turned sharply in the direction of his fiancée sitting next to him. "I'm literally sitting right here, babe."

"Yes, and you're doing it so well," she said, dropping a kiss on his cheek before pointing at the camera. "What happened, Fanny?"

"Why do you assume something happened?" Fanny asked, pulling her knees to her chest as she sat on the studio floor in front of the laptop. It was an unseasonably chilly morning for the last weekend in April. When she had gone out for coffee at Georgia's this morning, a light frost had blanketed the blossoming cherry trees with sparkles and she had needed to duck back in to the studio. To grab a jacket, of course, not because she had seen Law's Jeep parked in front of the cheese shop. "He could be in the bathroom or on a job."

"But he's not, is he?" Collette shook her head sadly. "I knew it was too good to be true, but I let my guard down and started thinking about how cute it would be to raise our babies together."

"Our what now?" Keith's eyes grew as wide as saucers as he planted a startled gaze on Collette's belly. "Don't do that to me, babe. My body's still on Eastern Standard Time and it's morning there. Way too early for jump scares."

"Just like to keep you on your toes." Collette patted his knee. "Well, speaking of being on your toes, let's get this dance party started. I've got a promo shoot with a photographer from *Hello! Magazine* in an hour. But if you think you're getting out of this conversation, you're dreaming. After we dance for you, we're saving the last fifteen minutes of this session for story time and I expect all the gory details of what happened between you and Mr. Muscles."

She stood up and backed away from the camera as Keith took a moment to silently flex his biceps and nod approvingly as if in validation.

Fanny watched, especially impressed with Keith. She knew between games and training and press he didn't have a lot of free time, and dancing clearly didn't come naturally to him. What he lacked in ease, however, he made up for with hard work and a good sense of humor that came out whenever his eyes twinkled down at Collette. Even with a few mistakes and a stumble on the last dip, they not only still put on a genuinely enjoyable performance to watch, but were so in sync with each other that they glided past the missteps without stopping the flow of the movement. That was what a good partnership looked like; it wasn't about perfection or getting through the routine without errors. It was about communication, trust, knowing each other's weaknesses and strengths, and balancing them out with your own. When they finished with a kiss, Fanny clapped her hands loudly.

"That was amazing!" she said. "Now, Keith, just remember that in the dip, you have to really support her back with your left arm. She's gonna be in heels on the day and it might throw off her balance. Your job is to stay grounded and really bend your knees so she has the freedom to arch her back and stretch her leg, all right?"

"Got it." He nodded soberly.

"I'm flying back to Toronto next week and

we'll have three days together there before we fly to LA for the wedding," Collette added, dabbing at the sweat on her forehead with the back of her hand. "We'll make sure to practice the dance with our shoes on a few times so we get the feel of it. Now," she said, sitting cross-legged on the floor and tugging at Keith's hand to pull him down next to her. "Tell me why you and Law are no longer together."

"We were never 'together' like that," Fanny said using air quotes around the word she echoed from her friend. "He was only my dance partner for your first dance. That's it. Well, and we're doing the dance at the Crystal Hill Dance Studio's recital in two weeks, but then that's it. For us and for the studio apparently."

"Why?" Collette asked, tipping her head to one side.

"Because Madame Rousseau is closing the studio," Fanny explained. "She's getting older and has health issues and can't keep it going anymore. It's a shame because the dance studio is right next to this gorgeous classic theater. Literally the ideal setup, but it's an old building and needs a lot of work. She almost sold the whole thing to this terrible chain gym owner from the next town over who was just going to bulldoze most of it and keep a few of the studio spaces for, like, hot yoga or something." Fanny wrinkled her nose, then shook her head. "Anyway, I found out that Law knew about the possibility of the sale the whole time and didn't tell me. He's not going to work with the guy anymore—in fact, he actively stopped the sale—but we got into a big fight because he wants me to stay here and take over the studio for Madame Rousseau when we have this amazing opportunity to go on tour with Murray. Did Murray tell you about it?"

"He did." Collette nodded, then her forehead wrinkled with concern. "Just out of curiosity, why don't you want to stay and take over the studio? You seem really passionate about it."

"It just seems so…final," Fanny said, sitting on the floor of the studio and sliding her legs in front of her, then leaning forward and resting her chin in her hands. "When my performing career ended so abruptly, it broke my heart. The idea of living in a small town and teaching dance felt like settling. It's like the saying, 'Those who can't do, teach.'" She sighed heavily. "I worked so long and hard to become a professional dancer. It's easier just to leave the dance world behind entirely than accept that I can't do it anymore. But when I got the idea to go on tour and present the first dance choreography with Law, it seemed like the perfect way to exit the stage, so to speak."

"And Law doesn't want to go on tour?" Keith asked. "I gotta say, I don't blame him. The only reason I'm doing this whole thing is for Collette and it's literally giving me anxiety sweats at night."

Collette grimaced. "It's true. He had to ask the hotel for extra sheets."

Fanny straightened her back as she sat up and fidgeted with a bobby pin that had come loose in her bun. "Well, he was willing to go on tour, but not the whole time. His whole family is here and his business, and now that I'm saying it out loud, I might have been a little bit unreasonable. That doesn't excuse him for not telling me the truth about the sale of the dance studio, though," she said, crossing her arms over her chest and pointing her toes down toward the camera. "What kind of future could I possibly have with a guy who lets me down like that? It's Jason all over again."

"First of all, Jason was a narcissistic jerk who took advantage of the crush you had on him to serve his own career." Collette pointed a finger at the camera. "He never did a single thing unless it was for his own benefit. Law took time out of his schedule to do this dance with you without getting anything in return, and he's willing to leave his hometown and go on tour with you at least for a few stops even though he's about as enthusiastic a dancer as Keith is."

"True story," Keith said.

"Second of all—" Collette leaned forward toward the camera and gave Fanny a loving smile "—you *like* him. And I get why that scares you. You went to boarding school for dance at, what, fourteen? Joined the ballet company at eighteen, and you've toured all over the world. All on your own."

"That's normal for dancers." Fanny frowned. "You have to learn to be independent at a young age. Sacrificing time with family, all the normal small-town high school stuff, that's just something you get used to when you choose this lifestyle. You have to be strong enough to do it on your own or you don't make it as a professional performer."

"But you did make it," Collette pointed out. "Nothing will take that experience away from you. Taking over the studio you're clearly invested in and having a relationship with a guy you obviously care about isn't a consolation prize."

"You didn't lose the game," Keith chimed in. "Our coaches are still part of the team even though they're off the ice. When our team wins the Stanley Cup, they get rings the same as we do."

"That's such a great example, babe." Collette turned and smiled at him with eyes that might as well have had emoji sparkles coming out of them. "I'm glad you gave me a ring, too, even though I don't know the first thing about the sportsball you play."

"I mean, the first thing you should know is we don't use a ball," Keith said with a laugh. "See, Fanny? We compromise. Sounds like Law was willing to do that with you. The question is, would moving to Crystal Hill and taking over the dance studio be a compromise you can live with or a sacrifice you're going to resent?"

His insight impressed Fanny even more than his effort on the dance floor. In the beginning, she had questioned what a creative, artistic person like Collette might have in common with a professional athlete who didn't know Shakespeare from Shake Shack. Now she got it. "It's not really an option, either way. Even if Madame Rousseau sold me the business for the same amount as the commission I'm getting from your wedding planner, I couldn't afford the renovations that the building needs."

Collette stared into Keith's eyes for a moment, then whispered behind her hand into his ear. He scrubbed a hand over his dark beard, then nodded in response. Collette's eyes lit up as she turned back to the camera.

"What if the money was raised to save the studio?" she asked with an innocent lilt to her voice that Fanny knew full well meant she was plotting something. "Putting the whole Law situation aside, is running the dance school a second act you could see being passionate enough about to make you stay in Crystal Hill?"

Instantly, Fanny knew the answer to that question. Even worse, she knew that Collette knew she knew and she jutted her chin in Keith's direction. "You do know you're marrying a woman who is annoyingly always right, don't you? You sure you're ready for a lifetime of that?"

Keith gazed down at his fiancée with a look that sent longing pangs through Fanny's midsection. "With all my heart."

"But whatever you're planning, Collette," Fanny continued, ignoring the image of Law's eyes flashing like a morning sky in her head, "I am not going to let you write a blank check for my future. That's not what our friendship is. I mean, getting paid for my time by your wedding coordinator is a job. Having a friend like you in my corner is more important to me than anything. I'll figure it out somehow."

After she hung up the call, she started to close the laptop, then an alert dinged with a new email notification. She closed her eyes and inhaled, holding her breath before she pushed the laptop back open and opened the tab for her email. It was probably Murray asking for an answer about the tour. She still wanted to do it, but looking back at the irrational way she had dumped all her emotions out on Law, there was no guarantee he would be willing to give up any more of his time for her than he already had. Despite his willingness to be humiliated on the dance floor, he had his pride. It was one of the things they shared, along with the likelihood of both their photos being pinned up in the doorway of Big Joe's Diner with big red X's and the words "Banned for Life" written above their images.

The email wasn't from the wedding planner, though. It was from her former partner, Jason. Apparently, he was on a break from touring and back in New York. He wanted to know if she would meet him for lunch after he was done teaching a masterclass at Marymount Manhattan. There was something he needed to talk to her about and it was time-sensitive.

Well, there was something she needed, too, and he might just be the person to help her get it.

CHAPTER SEVENTEEN

Lawson walked out of Weill Cornell Medicine Neuromuscular Center in Manhattan feeling better than he had in a long time, despite the fact that his arm was killing him from the blood draws and all the pulling and twisting the doctors had made him do during the tests that morning.

He flexed his wrist as he pulled out his phone to search for a deli nearby. Sure, if he bought lunch on top of paying for parking it would add on extra expenses to a consult that was probably already going to cost him an arm and a leg. But since he was now staring down the barrel of another medical procedure, Law figured he might as well treat himself to a decent meal. Tony's DiNapoli was a few blocks' walk down the street, and while the restaurant only served family-style, he was hungry enough to eat several servings of baked ziti bolognese all by himself. It would be good fuel for the long drive back to

Crystal Hill, and nothing soothed the pangs of a wounded heart like homemade pasta baked and topped with good melted cheese.

Fanny hadn't spoken to him in almost ten days. When the doctor told him that there was a new, implantable technology that would help with the healing of his nerve graft that had become inflamed and was causing all his pain, she was the first person he wanted to call. But the way her eyes had cut him like shards of green obsidian—Georgia's boyfriend had done a lecture on volcanic geology two months ago and the sample he had shown was an exact match for their hue—was enough to make him slide his phone back into his pocket. He didn't blame her for being angry when he looked at it from her perspective. No matter how many times he had tried to tell her about the sale with Napolitano, something had always gotten in the way and he had used that as a convenient excuse not to do the hard thing and risk her rejecting him over it. The worst part of everything she had said to him was the accuracy of it. He did give up at the first sign things might not go easily or go his way at all. He had done it with woodworking after his injury, the first time she had asked him to dance with her, and every time she tried to teach him a new move his first instinct was to assume he couldn't do it and try for something easier. No wonder she felt like she couldn't trust him.

As he waited to cross the street, he glanced over at a coffee shop with a bright blue awning over the door and a rack of pastries in the window that made his already rumbling stomach increase the volume of its demands. Maybe a little dessert before lunch would hit the spot. He had some tough decisions to mull over and mulling always went down easier with a chocolate hazelnut tart. Turning to cross south instead of continuing west, he merged with a crowd of tourists clutching Roosevelt Island guidebooks and anxiously checking their watches. Once he stepped onto the curb, however, he stopped cold when he got close enough to look beyond the cream-filled puffs on the top rack.

Sitting across from each other in a cozy corner booth were Fanny and a guy who looked vaguely familiar. Law took out his phone and leaned against a bench, trying to look casual as he squinted to get a closer look, and then it hit him. The guy was her former partner, the one whose carelessness was responsible for her career-ending injury. The hand not holding the phone clenched at his side.

What was she doing having coffee with this

guy? The guy was leaning forward, talking at a rapid-fire pace and gesturing expressively with his hands. Gosh darn it, even this guy's hand movements were coordinated. Law had made the unfortunate choice to look up videos of the two of them dancing together in the beginning, when he and Fanny had first joined forces, and regretted it even more now. The two of them moved so beautifully together, it was like watching classical sculptures in a museum come to life. As he looked at them in person, their chemistry was even more apparent. She couldn't take her eyes off him.

The obvious conclusion was that since she still planned to go on tour with the wedding planner, Law was out entirely and Captain Jazz Hands was in.

He turned on his heel and stood on the corner facing northwest: the direction of Crystal Hill, where he would drive back to later today and start reorganizing his life all over again. Unable to resist turning his head to get one more look at Fanny, he watched her nod intently before taking a sip of coffee from her oversize mug, and something stabbed at his heart. Most of all, he wanted her to be happy. If that was with this guy and his hair that was far too perfectly coiffed to not be at least a portion hairpiece, then so be it. But he knew, knew deep down, that she belonged in Crystal Hill. She fit there, with the people there who had embraced her creativity and sardonic humor and her tender guidance of their children into the world of the arts. It was the same way she fit perfectly in his arms each time they met in their dance frame as Harry Connick Jr. crooned at them from the sound system.

It figured. He finally knew what he wanted to do with his future and where and with whom, and the cornerstone to all of it was leaving. He had taken his shot with her and she had run away from him again. This time right into the arms of another man who could actually keep up with her step for step instead of stepping on her toes. As if adding insult to injury, as Law stepped off the curb to cross the street once more, he stubbed his toe and fell straight into the crosswalk, nearly missing being trampled by a group of children in matching field trip T-shirts.

Story of his life.

It was almost dark by the time he made it back to his trailer, yet Law parked his Jeep and walked over to the foundation of the house he could see so clearly in his mind even though at the moment it was still just a rectangle of pavers. Sighing deeply, he started to pick them up one at a time and carry them over to his wheelbarrow. There was no point now. All the money he had earmarked for building the house would need to go toward paying off the inevitable flood of medical bills after his surgery. Besides, if he couldn't have a life here in Crystal Hill with Fanny, he didn't see the point in building a family home anymore. The family he was staying here for had homes of their own and the family he wanted was going on tour with Gene Smelly from the coffee shop. And where did that leave him? The bachelor, the fun uncle, the guy who fixed everyone else's problems except his own. That guy didn't need a big house. A trailer where he and his woodworking tools would live happily ever after would be plenty of space for that guy.

Law picked up the last stone and heaved it into the wheelbarrow with a grunt, then stood up straight and stared at the darkening horizon over the treetops. The quiet of twilight enveloped him, and as the first stars made their appearance in the lavender-gray sky, he couldn't hide the truth even in the rapidly growing darkness.

He didn't want to be that guy anymore.

The next morning he woke up not to his alarm

reminding him of the time for his dance rehearsal with Fanny, but to the alert for a handyman job in town. Although he had started to put in bids for GC work, he would still need the handyman wages in the meantime as supplemental income. The doctor had told him he would need at least four weeks of occupational therapy after the procedure to heal his graft before he could get back to woodworking, and while Lucas kept him well supplied with dairy products, man could not live by cheese alone. Well, Lucas could, but he was an anomaly and should be studied.

When he saw that the call had come from the dance studio, he leaped out of bed with uncommon grace and didn't even trip over the pile of shoes and clothes he had left despondently on the floor last night when he had returned to his trailer.

It wasn't Fanny who had called him, though, and while he was disappointed to see Madame Rousseau waiting for him at the top of the stairs, he couldn't say he was surprised. Fanny was probably still in some five-star Manhattan hotel with Fred Asnore. Hmm, that one needed work.

"Law, you got here fast," Madame Rousseau commented, looking down at her watch, then back up at him. "This wasn't an emergency. I hope you didn't rush to get here or anything."

Law struggled to appear to breathe evenly although he had basically sprinted out of his car and taken the steps two at a time. "No, erm, not at all. I was just…in the area," he lied, crossing his arms over his chest to hide any burgeoning sweat stains on his light blue T-shirt. "What do you need?"

"The barre in Studio B is squeaking," she said, pointing through the door at the studio. "I was hoping you could get in there and grease her up a bit."

"Oh." With all of the problems in this building, that was an easy fix. "I have some WD-40 in my Jeep. Let me go get it."

He walked—no point in running this time—back down the stairs and grabbed the can from the back. When he returned, he didn't see Madame Rousseau in the studio that needed work, but the sound of her voice echoed through the wall from the adjoining Studio A, along with the clacking of pointe shoes interspersed with the occasional rapping of the dance teacher's cane on the floor. The recital was coming up in less than a week, and while the students had their classes and rehearsals in the evenings after school, the professional guest artists who would be performing practiced during the day.

Law got to work on the barre, trying to block out the rehearsal sounds. It was just another reminder that in less than a week he and Fanny would dance together for the last time and then she would be gone for good. But when the floating melody of the piano stopped, he couldn't help overhearing Madame Rousseau lecturing her dancers.

"Misty, remember the lift doesn't start just when you run and leap into his arms," she said, her raspy voice unusually loud for some reason today. "Before you begin anything, you make the decision to commit with everything you have in you. It's not enough to trust his strength and hope he catches you. You have to be all in before you take the first step. If you hesitate, if you don't put all of your energy into this, that's when you get hurt. Now let's try again from the supported pirouette."

He paused midtwist of the grease-soaked rag. Was that what he was doing now? Was he hesitating instead of going all in with Fanny? Yes, she had been angry with him in the moment and told him to forget about the tour. But this was what they did with each other. They teased and pushed and challenged each other, whether it was with a new dance step or a party where she didn't know anyone besides him. Together they made a great team because they refused to let each other settle for less than everything. If he really believed in their future together, here in Crystal Hill, then he had to convince her he believed in them as dance partners. That was the key to her heart, her passion.

Pushing on the barre to test it for squeaks, Law tucked the rag into the waistband of his jeans and picked up the can of WD-40. He went into the lobby preparing to sit on one of the little pink chairs as long as it took for her to come back, even if it meant he wouldn't be able to move again for at least forty-eight hours afterward. The door to the studio opened and he started to stand, but the chair meant for a ten-year-old backside was now stuck to his own thirty-two-year-old backside. Quickly, he—and the chair—sat back down and he crossed his legs in an attempt to appear casual.

However, the person he had planned to wait for an eternity in his plastic pink prison wasn't who appeared at the top of the steps. Instead, it was Marco, Joe Kim and Silas Stephenson, owner of Stephenson's Jewelry and Antiques. The trio stood in front of him and returned his puzzled gaze.

"What are *you* doing here?" Marco asked, tipping his silvery head to one side and lifting an eyebrow at his choice of seating. "And why are you sitting in that tiny seat? Is there some sort of Goldilocks-themed challenge the kids are doing these days?"

"Madame Rousseau called me here to do some repairs to the studio," Law replied with as much dignity as he could muster from his minuscule throne. "I could ask you the same question."

"We're here for the audition," Joe said, brushing a questionable-looking red stain off the front of his apron. "Fanny's been out all over town this morning handing out flyers. She's going on a tour of wedding shows to prove that any guy can learn to ballroom dance at his wedding and she's looking for a partner. I assumed you had left town on another one of your adventures."

"Well, I haven't and I'm not going to," Law said. He shifted his hips from side to side and at last broke free enough to stand and scan the line of men in front of him for answers. "But I don't understand. I thought she was getting back together with her old dance partner for the tour. The professional guy."

"She's never getting back together with Jason." Apparently, the walls were thin enough for sound to bleed through all the way around, because Madame Rousseau poked her head out of the door of Studio A to interject. "She came back late last night after meeting up with him in the city. He had emailed her and asked to get together for coffee or something like that. Fanny only agreed because that life coach person told her she needed closure from the end of her dance career before she could make any plans for the future. She thought he was going to apologize for dropping and hurting her, but as usual, he was only thinking about himself. He heard through the grapevine about Fanny being hired by that fancy event planner—there's talk he might be in line to choreograph the Tony Awards this year—and Jason wanted to schmooze Fanny to put in a good word for him." Madame Rousseau's face cracked in a terrifyingly wicked smile. "I guess his career is going down the toilet and he can't get enough work to keep his equity card. Don't tell me karma isn't real."

Her head disappeared back behind the door and the lighthearted piano music started back up. Law's own head spun with the influx of new information, yet something still didn't seem right. He turned his head sharply to Joe.

"Joe, how are you going to leave the diner for

six months?" he asked as he twisted his lower back to get it to crack. "You're the owner and head chef. It was the main reason I couldn't go with her as her partner. I'm trying to get my business started here and plant some real roots in Crystal Hill, and being away that long would have made that almost impossible."

Joe scratched his head and made a confused face. "Six months? She told me it was only going to be two months and in early winter. The wedding planner told her that January through March are what they call 'bridal Christmas' in the industry because of all the proposals between actual Christmas and Valentine's Day. Those are the wedding shows with the highest attendance, so she's planning to hit up only those and do the rest as, like, Zoom calls on a big screen or something."

That timing would be perfect for Law's business. The major renovation and building projects around here always slowed during winter, and by then he would have built up some revenue that he could afford the break in productivity. Hope sprung up in his chest like a leak from a burst pipe, showering him with possibility. This was his chance. He had to show Fanny that he could help her not only get closure from her past, but inspiration for a new life here with him. The question was: How did he show her that he was ready to commit to this partnership on and off the dance floor?

Suddenly it hit him. Fanny was looking for something to get passionate about in her second act, a way to contribute to the dance world even if she could no longer perform. Something that would give her a purpose to stay here in Crystal Hill beyond being with him, because he knew he hadn't earned her trust enough to get her to leap right into his arms.

"Guys," he said, spreading his hands out to them with his palms turned up. "I know I'm normally the one everyone calls for help fixing things, but I really messed up with Fanny and this time, I'm asking for help from you. We don't have a lot of time and it's going to involve risking deep, public humiliation, so I totally understand if your answer is no."

Silas rubbed his chin with one hand and twisted his head to look at the other two men standing to his right. "What do you think? Should we help him out?"

"I think that sacrificing your honor to help someone for the sake of love is the most noble expression of friendship," Marco said pushing his shoulders back and puffing out his chest.

"I mean, if you hadn't come in and cleaned

out my grease trap while I was in Buffalo for the hot wing convention, my whole place would have gone up in smoke." Joe took one of Law's extended hands and shook it, clapping him on the back with the other before turning to face Marco and Silas. "And, you know, all that stuff Marco said, too."

Silas nodded. "We're in, Handyman Law. How can we help?"

Law grinned. "You're going to have to show me your best dance moves," he said, performing one of the three-step turns Fanny had taught him, nearly running into the wall in the process. "Can you guys hang out for an hour in Studio B? We're going to have to be cool about it, though. I want it to be a surprise for Fanny at the dress rehearsal next week."

"We can be cool," Silas said, then pointed at Law's jeans. "But you might want to remove the sparkly unicorn sticker stuck to your butt if you want to say the same for yourself."

CHAPTER EIGHTEEN

As Keith and Collette took to the floor for their first dance, Fanny tried her best to keep cool.

This was already an uphill climb given the wedding took place outdoors in Los Angeles on the first weekend of May. There was a sheer canopy over the dance floor, which had been installed on the grounds of the state park for the event. Eden Gardens, with its verdant overhang of oak and willow trees, perfumed gardens and the trickle of fountains in the background, absolutely lived up to the paradise its name evoked, yet no atmosphere could change the fact that it was hot.

Fanny took another sip of ice water with cucumber slices floating inside it and looked around. No one else was sweating profusely through their black tie formalwear or was holding their thick hair off their neck to keep the curls from turning into pasted tentacles. She thought longingly of the fresh breeze that seemed to constantly funnel down from the Adirondacks through downtown Crystal Hill, and the shade provided by the evergreens watching silently over Law's peaceful plot of land. Then she shook her head and forced herself to focus on the dance floor. This was what she had been missing, wasn't it? The excitement of travel, the glamour of people dressing in their best whether it was to a theater or a wedding. When she went on tour with the wedding planner, she could finally get back to a life that provided the thrill of new scenery and new adventures instead of the same place and people day after day.

If she went on tour. Fanny had passed out flyers to all the men who had attended her first audition, as well as pasted them all over town, but no one showed up to the audition this time. Since she couldn't do the dance by herself and she wouldn't bring herself to ask Law to join her—not that he would say yes, anyway, after the way she had yelled at him—there was a good chance the tour wasn't going to happen for her at all. It had been the one thing she had hoped would give her the peace she needed to walk away from the dance world with any sort of resolution. It wasn't like her meeting with Jason had provided any closure. All he had wanted was to see if she could give him an in with Murray before rehearsals started for the

Tony Awards ceremony. Once she had informed him that as far as she knew, he didn't have anything to do with the ceremony, casting or otherwise, Jason had quickly tossed down a couple of bills for the coffee and left the café on the Lower East Side fast enough to leave a Jason-shaped cutout in the wall.

Fanny sighed and allowed her shoulders to slump forward. Yes, it had been a beautiful wedding and she shouldn't be complaining about any of it—the five-star hotel Keith and Collette had put her up in as a thank-you, the window-shopping outing she had taken on Rodeo Drive yesterday. Yet everything she thought would lift her spirits only made her miss Crystal Hill more. She missed the quiet of walking down Jane Street where the only traffic noise was the birds chirping from the crabapple trees in bloom. She missed the yogurt from the dairy shop that had become her new favorite breakfast, along with a strong coffee and a pastry from Georgia's. There was, of course, one person she missed most of all, but she wouldn't say it to him. Law had probably moved on to the next woman waiting in line for the town's most eligible bachelor the second she had left Big Joe's Diner. He would never change, would never be the guy she could trust with her heart.

He simply couldn't understand what it meant to have a passion that was your guiding force through life and all its hardships.

When the intro to "It Had to Be You" started up, Fanny's feet moved instinctively under the table. She and Law had danced together to this so many times, she could have sworn she could smell the combination of wood shavings and soap that clung to him in an almost irresistible scent that rivaled any of Jason's expensive colognes. She forced herself to straighten up and pay attention to the dance floor. In a masterstroke of timing, twinkle lights lit up over the canopy as soon as Collette finished her walk around and twirled into Keith's arms. The other guests murmured in surprise and delight, but Fanny kept her eyes trained on the couple, her hands twitching reflexively with each turn. She even felt her chin turn up to the ceiling the same time as Collette's when Keith brought her up in the lift. The couple held each other's eyes as they walk-stepped back and forth, and when Collette leaned into Keith's side just before the dip, Fanny knew he would support her through whatever came their way. A sharp longing to have that same support from the only man who had looked at her the same way Keith looked at Collette filled her like the air she breathed.

The music trailed off and as Fanny swallowed back the lump in her throat and clapped for the couple, a notification on her phone dinged. She checked it and frowned. It was a text from Madame Rousseau.

Thank you for sending your crew to the theater to start building the sets. Good luck on the procedure today!

Fanny read the text twice. Was Madame Rousseau okay? Although she was struggling with the physical effects of her COPD, as far as she knew the woman's mind was still razor-sharp. She tapped a text back, ignoring the clinking of glasses around her.

This is Fanny. Are you all right? The text you just sent me was confusing.

A moment later, she got a text back.

Sorry, dear. Meant to send that to Lawson. My old fingers fumble on these tiny phone keypads.

Fanny frowned. So, Madame Rousseau was on texting terms with Law, now? She texted a quick reply.

Okay, just checking.

Then she added:

Out of curiosity, what kind of procedure is Law having done? Not a big deal if you don't know. I don't really care. Just wondering.

The three dots that indicated Madame was typing seemed to last an eternity before another text popped up.

He's having work done on his injured arm. He saw a specialist in Manhattan this past week who could do an implantable treatment that will fix the pain he's been having. He plans to get back into woodworking and add that as a special service to his general contractor's package. If I was able to keep going with the studio, I'd have him build new sets for our recitals. He's one of a kind, that boy.

Fanny set the phone down on the table. The other guests leaped to their feet and rushed the dance floor as the first notes of "Shout" started up, but for the first time in her life, she didn't feel like dancing. He had actually listened to her, getting his arm fixed and following through on his passion even if it meant another painful, expensive procedure that may or may not work. Now that she was thinking about it, Law always listened to her. He followed her instructions and corrected his moves when they were rehearsing, he paid attention to her story at the baby shower, he showed up when she needed him, even when she had told him there wasn't anything in it for him including a future together. That was the guy Lawson Carl was now. He wasn't the same commitment-phobic Lothario he had been ten years ago, and from what she'd learned about him over the past several weeks, that might never have been who he really was anyway. All that charm and the way he raced all over town to fix his neighbors' broken pipes and slow Wi-Fi was a cover for the fact that he felt like he wasn't good enough. It was why he second-guessed every move and why he played the field. He was terrified of letting the people of Crystal Hill down, so terrified of it that he had said no to going on a six-month tour with her because he wanted to be there for them. That was the opposite of commitment-phobic. He loved his town, his family, the beautiful art he had been able to share with them.

And she was starting to think that she might love those same things.

Almost as much as she loved him.

Keith and Collette walked over to the table where Fanny sat, arms around each other's waists. Collette looked gorgeous in her reception gown, a sequin-covered, strapless ballgown with a long slit up one side. Her hair was down in long blond waves with rhinestone star combs pulling it away from her face, yet what shone more than all the sequins and diamonds were her eyes that she couldn't take off her new husband.

"You two were amazing out there." Fanny stood to give both of them a hug, then pulled away to watch them beaming with pride at each other. "I felt like a proud mom watching her kid at their first dance recital."

Collette pulled her gaze away from Keith long enough to point a finger at Fanny. "Hey, speaking of which, when is the dance recital at Crystal Hill? We have a stopover in JFK on our flight back from our honeymoon in Paris, and if the timing worked out, we thought we could take an extra few days and drive up to Crystal Hill to see it."

"It's next Sunday, so one week from tomorrow," Fanny said, fiddling with the tennis bracelet on her wrist. "I mean, it's not like it's Radio City or anything, so if you can't make it, you're not missing the show of the century. It really is amazing quality for a small-town dance studio, though. Madame Rousseau has coached dancers from all over the world, so she always gets great guest dancers and the kids are incredible. She's inspired them so much. I've never seen little kids who are that eager to come to dance class."

"Fanny, correct me if I'm wrong, but you sound like you really love this place," Collette said, putting a hand gently on Fanny's arm. "And I bet a part of why those kids are so excited to come to dance class is because of you. You're a fantastic teacher."

"Look at what you've taught me." Keith grinned. He hooked his right hand under the suspender of his tailored vintage tuxedo and pulled it out like a vaudeville performer. "I had so much fun doing this, I agreed to take ballroom dancing lessons with Collette. You and Law really inspired me."

"I think that was probably more Law's doing than mine." Fanny couldn't stop the broad smile from stretching across her face at the mention. "He really worked so hard even though I know for a fact dancing was the last thing on earth he wanted to be spending his time doing."

"And what do you want to spend your time doing?" Collette asked. "If affording the renovations wasn't an issue, would you take over the studio in Crystal Hill?"

"Yes." The way the answer flew out of her mouth before she had taken time to think it caught even Fanny by surprise. Still, it was true. She loved the town and the kids in her classes, and every time she thought about leaving for even six months of a tour, homesickness rose up and grabbed her by the throat "It's a moot point, though. Even with the generous commission from choreographing your wedding, I don't have enough money saved up for that kind of expense. The building needs a lot of work and I would want to do it justice."

Keith and Collette exchanged mischievous glances. "We might have some information that will help," Keith said, a wide smile breaking through his freshly trimmed beard.

"After our last Zoom session with you, we had a feeling this was where you were leaning," Collette said. "So we added a quick fundraising link to our wedding website that was only visible to invited guests, which you, as one of Murray's contractors, wouldn't be able to access. It said that if anyone hadn't yet gotten us a wedding gift, then as an alternative we would love for them to contribute to the Save the Crystal Hill Dance Studio Fund because of how you've inspired us to get even closer as a couple through these dance lessons." She nudged Keith with her hip and he pulled an envelope out of his back pocket before handing it to Fanny.

"People were very generous," he said with a wink.

Fanny collapsed back into her chair, speechless. "Guys, I—I don't know what to say. Thank you just doesn't seem like enough." Her eyes filled with grateful tears and she dabbed at the corners with her fingers. "I never cry, not even when I've danced on broken toes and sprained ankles. This nondancer life has me going soft."

Collette released her hold on Keith's waist to pull up the chair next to Fanny and sit next to her, grabbing her hands. "You will always be a dancer, no matter what any former partner or life coach tells you. That doesn't mean you can't love other things…or people, too." She ducked her chin down and looked Fanny directly in the eyes. "Happiness doesn't have to be earned through sacrifice or pain. You deserve joy without any strings attached and I think you've found it in Crystal Hill. Fighting for your passion is admirable, but there's also nothing wrong with accepting the gifts life offers you along the way. There's purpose in that, too." Keith put his hand on her shoulder and she squeezed it, the giant diamond on her finger catching the spark of the lights overhead.

Fanny set the envelope on the table next to her phone, then looked back at the couple. "I know I had planned to stay for brunch tomorrow, but would you mind too much if I tried to catch an earlier flight back home?"

Because that was what Crystal Hill was for her. It was home. It was friends and family and a sense of finally letting her hair down after years of tight buns and bobby pins. It was a man who could take a plain piece of wood and turn it into something beautiful.

"Of course," Collette said before standing and pulling Fanny up along with her. "But not before we get you out on the dance floor, lady. Come on and show these folks how it's done."

Fanny allowed her friend to drag her out to the floor and even though she had fun, dancing just didn't feel right anymore without her true partner by her side.

The next day when she returned to Crystal Hill after snagging a seat on the first flight out that morning, the first place she drove to was Law's property. Instead of seeing him puttering around with his pavers, scratching the stubble on his chin in a way that was inexplicably appealing and completely oblivious to how attractive he was, he wasn't there. Neither were the pavers. The lot had been cleared out. All that was left in the flattened grass was the outline of the house, the future he had wanted for himself. The emptiness broke her heart.

Had he given up on his beautiful plan entirely? Squinting across the field, she saw that the lights were off in his trailer, too. If he had just had the procedure done on his arm, she wouldn't have thought he would be out and about doing handyman work so soon. The idea that maybe he was out on a date with someone else struck her with a new vision of her own future, one in which she settled in Crystal Hill and took over the studio, yet had to watch as Law fell in love with and married some other woman here in town. As much as she hoped he was as interested in her as before, Fanny knew as well as anyone there were no guarantees, especially when you were trusting your dreams to someone else's hands. Out in LA she had been so sure about wanting to come back here, to take over for Madame Rousseau and go on a limited tour with Law as her dance partner. The question she needed answering now was, if she couldn't have that life with him, would she still want it for herself? And more specifically, would it be enough for her to move on from the past she still mourned?

Until she could answer that, she needed to keep her distance from Law because the second she looked into those eyes, all her well-honed dancer's discipline would fly out the window.

As soon as she got back into town, she started to trudge wearily up the steps to her little apartment.

Madame Rousseau was just finishing locking up the doors to the studios and turned to stop her. "Fanny dear, how was the wedding?"

"It was…eventful," Fanny answered, then she rubbed her eyes and shook her head. "I mean, it was really great. Collette looked beautiful and the dance was perfect. If ever there was a couple that embodied 'meant to be,' it's those two."

"Eventful," Madame Rousseau echoed thoughtfully, playing with the gilded top of her cane. "Does that mean you've come to a decision about what your second act is going to be?"

"I'm a lot closer than I was," Fanny said. "I just want to take some time this week to really be sure. By the recital on Saturday I'll have some answers for you, hopefully."

"Don't forget the dress rehearsal is on Friday evening at the theater," Madame Rousseau reminded her. "Do you have a costume picked out for your dance with Law?"

Fanny clapped a hand to her forehead. "Gah, no. I'm sorry. In all the craziness of the last two weeks, I completely forgot."

"Don't worry." Madame Rousseau waved her hand and her bracelets jangled. "I'll find something for you. In the meantime, I need you to do something for me this week."

"What is it?"

"There's a crew that's going to be working on the sets at the theater during the afternoons this week," Madame Rousseau said. She dropped her keys into the pocket of her long cardigan and walked across the lobby to look up to the step where Fanny stood. "Do you think you could stay there and supervise them, say, between one and three o'clock every day this week? That's the time of day I really need to lie down and rest so I can get through leading rehearsals in the evenings."

Fanny shrugged. "Of course. Anything for you, Madame."

"Oh, good," Madame Rousseau said before turning and heading down the stairs leading to the exit. "Now you go up and get some rest yourself. Traveling always wears you out, so be sure to get plenty of sleep. We've got a big week ahead of us."

"Good night, Madame," Fanny called after her. After she had watched to make sure Madame Rousseau made it down the steps and to her car, she turned and headed back up to her apartment, leaning on the handrail more heavily with each step.

She was tired, but it wasn't from the trip. She was tired of trying to make decisions, planning, balancing the pain of her past with the increasing weight of the future. She was tired of doing it on her own, and by *it*, she meant life. Watching Keith and Collette in person all day yesterday had made at least one thing perfectly clear. Fanny was ready for someone to be her partner through everything, the simple transition steps, the soaring lifts, the stumbles, all of it, and she wasn't talking about dance anymore. A life without her passion would always be unacceptable to her.

A life without love suddenly felt unbearable.

CHAPTER NINETEEN

Law donned his starched, white button-down shirt with more eagerness than he had ever felt for his most worn-in T-shirt and his softest fleece hoodie.

Tonight was the dress rehearsal for the recital and he would finally get to see Fanny again. All week he had hoped to run into her at the studio while he was there rehearsing with the guys. He even had a cover story meticulously planned in case she saw what they were doing and began to ask questions. Okay, so his cover story was simply that they were goofing off in between repairs to the floorboards, so not exactly Agatha Christie-level stuff, but his efforts had been pointless anyway. He hadn't seen so much as a flutter of one of her trademark filmy skirts all week. It was as if she had been a fairy he had dreamed up, flitting past him in a dream and disappearing the second he awoke.

As he straightened his collar in the mirror, a knock sounded on the door of his trailer.

"It's open," he called over his shoulder, still focused on his reflection in the mirror. Everything had to be perfect tonight, from his hair to the shoes that were scuffed just right on the soles, but shone like a mirror on top.

His brother, Lucas, opened the door. Chrysta was standing behind him, holding a squirming Bell.

"Whooo, don't you look snazzy," said Chrysta, weaving her head to one side to appraise Law while trying not to get smacked by her toddler's flailing hands. "Yes, baby, I know you're excited to see Uncle Law, but can we try to be cool about it? This is like trying to control a fangirling octopus."

"Well, then, let me take care of that." Law smiled and turned away from the mirror to cross the small living room and take Bell out of Chrysta's arms. "She's just getting her groove on." He took Bell's little hand in his and spun her around humming. The baby grinned back at him with eyes lit up like candles and giggled. Law laughed right back and nodded at Chrysta. "Look at her. She's a natural. We've got ourselves a future prima ballerina right here."

"Let's get her walking before you buy her tiny

pointe shoes, okay?" Lucas said. "Speaking of dance lessons, how are things going with you and Fanny?"

Law stuck his tongue out and made a silly face at his niece before answering. "I haven't seen her since our fight at Big Joe's, which I'm sure you all heard about through the Crystal Hill gossip network." He dipped Bell into a baby-friendly version of the "Hollywood dip" and she squealed with laughter. "But I've got something up my sleeve for tonight that will show her how much I care about her and want her to stay. The decision is hers, though. I want her to be free to choose whatever makes her happy, so I've been trying to give her enough space to figure that out for herself, you know? Even if that's not being here with me."

The smile that Bell's cuteness had brought to his face faded at the thought. He meant what he said. Fanny's happiness was the most important thing in all of this. If she stayed because she felt like she owed it to him, then that wasn't right. Over the past month, he had learned a lot about himself from her. She had been right about him giving up too easily on himself, on not taking risks because he was afraid of what people might think about him if they didn't work out. But when he was with her, he felt like even if he messed up a step or landed flat on his butt, it was all right. Life felt lighter, easier now, because he was sharing all of himself with her. At the end of the day, she had taught him so much more than just three-step turns and lifts, and if she left town and never came back, he would still be grateful for that.

"This is a really pretty piece of wood," Chrysta said, picking up a large log of untreated cherry from his kitchen table. "What are you going to do with it?"

"Not sure yet," Law replied, melting like a scoop of gelato in July when Bell put her little head on his chest and closed her eyes as he swayed from side to side. If being the fun uncle felt this good, he couldn't imagine how incredible it would be when the baby was his own. And if that baby had Fanny's green eyes and sharp wit? That was a vision he could commit to without hesitation. "I have some ideas, though."

"We'd better head out," Lucas said, reaching his hands out and sliding the sleeping baby from Law's arms. "We're meeting Georgia and Malcolm at the theater after they drop Caroline off backstage."

"I didn't realize so many people came to watch the dress rehearsal," Law said, turning back to his reflection to dab at the small drool puddle on his chest. "I was at the school district office earlier signing my company's contract to redo the football stadium—they're naming the new one, the Michael Wright Memorial Stadium after Georgia's first husband who died six years ago—a bunch of parents talked about being there to watch."

"I think word got out that there would be a special performance tonight," Chrysta said, looking over her shoulder with a wink as she walked out the door. "I know I wouldn't want to miss it."

Law's stomach dropped as they closed the door behind them. This was getting very real and suddenly very public. If he put himself out there and Fanny still said no, he was about to be rejected in front of most of the town. Literally his worst nightmare.

But he knew if he didn't take this chance, he'd regret it. Today, tomorrow and definitely for the rest of his life.

As he waited in the wings of the theater, he could hear the rustling of a far larger crowd than he had ever planned to witness his grand gesture. Twisting his left hand around his right wrist, he found the bandage from the injection sticking out underneath his sleeve. It was still a little tender, yet his range of motion had already improved and the nerve pain had diminished almost entirely. As soon as his company was turning a profit, he would definitely be making a charitable contribution to the medical school at Cornell because whatever they had done was nothing short of miraculous. Now, if only they could come up with a treatment for the nerves that were tingling not with pain from an injury, but fear that what he was about to do would blow up in his face. He didn't have much more time to think about it, though, because the heavy, red velvet curtains slowly dragged to the side of the stage.

It was showtime.

Law walked onto the stage and found the *X* marked with tape in the center where he was supposed to stand. The lights were so bright he couldn't see anything but darkness out in the audience, and the silence broken only by a few whispers and the giggling of the little girls waiting backstage added to his panic that was quickly building into terror. This wasn't his first time on stage; he'd done plays in high school, played hockey in front of much larger crowds than this, and yet all he wanted in this moment was to run back to his foundation and hide behind a pile of his pavers.

Then Fanny walked onstage and hit her mark.

She wore a glittering white dress that flowed to just below her knees and her hair was down in waves across her shoulders. When she turned her head to look at him and her lips tilted up in a genuine, real smile, Law knew there was nothing even the scientists at Cornell could come up with that would be a better cure. She was everything he needed.

When the music started, however, the smile fell away from her face because the song wasn't "It Had to Be You."

It was "I Wanna Dance with Somebody" by Whitney Houston.

Shielding her eyes from the spotlight, Fanny started to wave at the sound engineer in the booth above the auditorium. Her attention was diverted when Joe, Marco and Silas joined Law onstage in a line. While Law was dressed in a white button-down shirt with an undone black tie that matched his black tuxedo pants, the others wore their own version of Sunday best. For Silas, it was a vintage powder-blue tuxedo with ruffles on the white shirt and matching blue bow tie, for Marco it was an all-black Armani suit with a red rose in the lapel, and for Joe, it was a brightly patterned Hawaiian shirt over khaki shorts and sandals over white knee socks.

The quartet formed a straight line and when

Whitney's iconic chorus began, they went into their routine, which was basically the steps Fanny had taught them at their audition: a box step, a three-step turn and the cha-cha step. As Law concentrated on keeping to the beat, he also kept one eye on Fanny, whose hands covered her mouth in either shock or horror, it was too early to tell which.

After the cha-cha step, the guys stepped to the background and swayed side to side while Caroline ran out onstage with a microphone and handed it to Law.

"Good luck," she whispered with a gap-toothed grin as she handed it to him.

"I thought you were supposed to say 'break a leg,'" he whispered back, taking the microphone.

"I was going to, but I didn't want you to get hurt again for real," she said, giving him a quick hug before running back into the wings.

Law shook his head and looked down, smiling, before he raised the microphone to his lips. "Folks, in case you hadn't guessed it, this little impromptu performance is not going to be an official part of the recital," he said over the music the sound engineer had lowered slightly for him. "But Miss Fanny has done so much for our town in her short time here, inspiring the kids with her love of dance, and even achieving the impossible—" he chuckled and swept a hand down his body "—turning this former hockey player with two left feet and a bum arm into an honest-to-goodness dancer. We wanted to show her not only how much we appreciate her, but how much we still need her services as dance teacher extraordinaire." He extended an arm out to Fanny and looked at her with pleading in his eyes that he didn't have to fake for the performance. "Madame Rousseau has tried for years to get more boys and men in town to join the studio and discover that dance is for everyone. If you're willing to take up the cause, we promise to do whatever we can to recruit a new generation of sturdy partners for your female dancers. Fanny, we're desperate. If you're not sure, look at these guys' best moves and tell me we don't need professional help."

He stepped to the side and the music grew louder as Silas strutted out of the line and struck a disco pose with one finger pointing to the sky and a hip jutted out at an awkward angle. After gyrating his hips to the beat, he proceeded to march like a drum line leader in a circle before retreating back to the line and allowing Marco to come forward and take the spotlight. Marco's hands went over his head and he clapped his hands completely off the beat while his feet stamped the ground as if there was a cockroach he was trying to smash. When it was Joe's turn, he jumped with both feet in the air then pretended to surf, one hand stretched out toward the audience, the other waving an imaginary lasso in the air.

The song reached its crescendo and the men formed their line once more, linked arms, and kicked their legs in front Rockette-style, although given that none of them could get their legs higher than knee-level, perhaps geriatric Rockette-style was more accurate. Finally, they ended their performance by kneeling on one knee—Law offered his elbow to assist Silas—and reaching into their back pockets to throw a shower of rose petals in Fanny's direction as the song faded into silence.

The silence didn't last more than a second or two because cheers and applause exploded from backstage and the auditorium seats. The thunderous volume took Law by surprise as he hadn't expected that many people to attend the dress rehearsal, and from onstage, there was no way of telling how many people were actually out there watching. For Pete's sake, it sounded like the whole town was in attendance. But even if that were the case, there was only one person whose reaction mattered to him.

Rising to his feet to stand, Law spoke into the microphone once more to her. "Clearly, this is a cry for help. Only you can take moves like… whatever that was—" he wagged a thumb over his shoulder at the guys behind him "—and transform them into men who aren't running in fear from the dance floor at every wedding and high school reunion. If you're at all considering staying in Crystal Hill to take over the dance studio, it would be a lifesaver not just for us, but for the future generations to avoid our sad, uncoordinated fates. We need you," he said out loud, then lowering the microphone, added quietly only to her, "I need you. Please stay."

Fanny brought her hands off her face. Her eyes shimmered, he hoped with happy tears, although it could just have been the lights. She crossed the stage and took the microphone, her hands brushing his for just a moment before she turned to the audience.

"Well, that was quite a performance, wasn't it?" The audience roared once more and she pivoted to face Law and his misfit gang of background dancers. "But I'm afraid I can't commit to staying until I see *your* best moves," she said, pointing straight at Law.

He lowered his chin and lifted his eyebrows in mock alarm as he jabbed a thumb at his chest and mouthed "Me?"

She bobbed her head in an exaggerated nod.

Reaching for the microphone, he turned and tossed it to Marco, who caught it with a wink before exiting offstage with the other guys. Law hooked his left thumb under his suspenders and walked backward two steps to resume his spot on the taped *X*. He looked up at the sound booth and gave a thumbs-up with his right hand. The orchestral introduction to "It Had to Be You" floated through the auditorium while Law said loud enough for her to hear over the music, "I can't do this without you, Fanny."

Blinking, she twisted her lips to one side then picked up her skirt with one hand and began her circle walk around Law right on cue. Even though they hadn't danced together in almost two weeks, it was like his body knew exactly what to do without having to think about it, which was good because all he could think was how he'd never seen anyone so beautiful in his entire life as the woman swirling into his arms. Her gaze never left his face, even during the lift, and her smile was brighter than any spotlight on the biggest stages in the world. They moved back and forth together in perfect harmony—

Law didn't trip over his own feet or even come close to stepping on her toes. When he lowered her into their final "Hollywood dip," it felt like they were the only two people in the Universe. He could have stayed in that perfect moment forever, but the illusion was shattered by applause, cheers and whistles from the crowd in the audience and all the young dancers who had gathered in the wings to watch.

Law brought Fanny slowly up from the dip and they stood with their arms around each other for another second before pulling apart. He bowed as she swept into a graceful curtsy before they left the stage hand in hand.

As the rehearsal continued as planned with the ballet classes performing variations from "The Sleeping Beauty," he pulled Fanny into a quiet corner next to a large painted tree that would be part of the set for the finale. It was so realistic that he almost felt like he was back in the woods next to his foundation—or where his foundation used to be before he had to tear it up to afford the procedure on his arm.

As if she could read his thoughts, Fanny gently reached for his right arm and rolled his sleeve over his elbow to skim her fingers along the bandage.

"How is it?" she asked, looking up at him with concern softening the sharp angles of her face.

"The incision site is still a little tender," he admitted, flexing his hand. "But the nerve pain was gone within the first twenty-four hours. It's unreal. I hadn't realized how present the pain was on a low level even just with normal movements until it went away. Over in Bingleyton, there's a great outpatient therapy clinic that specializes in nerve injuries. I had an evaluation with the PT and OT last week and they said I should be able to get back to woodworking by the end of the month."

"That's great to hear," she said. Her lips curved into a smile as she looked down and rolled the sleeve back over the bandage, then kept both her hands clasped over his. "Because I'm going to need you completely healed by this coming fall at the latest."

Law tipped his head to one side. "I thought you weren't going on tour until the winter," he said. "I mean, if you still want me to be your partner for it."

"I do," she replied softly, lifting her gaze to his and holding it as if she couldn't tear her eyes away from him for a second. "But I'm going to need your skills as a woodworker to build all-new sets for my production of *The Nutcracker* for Crystal Hill Dance Studio's Christmas show next year, and I'll need to see some working miniature models of your design if you want me to hire you as the studio's official general contractor for all its renovations going forward."

Law's breath stilled in his chest. He was afraid to let it out because it might wake him up from this scene he had dreamt so many times over the last month. "Does this mean you're staying? For good?"

"Yes," she said. "For good and for me. I realized this is what I want my second act to be. Dancing with you just now—" she gestured to the stage with her left hand, still holding his in her right "—that was the perfect way to say goodbye to my career as a performer on tour and a way of opening the door to a new beginning here with you. Law, I don't just need you to build sets and perform first dances with me on tour. I need you because I'm falling in love with you. You're perfect just the way you are, and I can't imagine doing any of this with anyone else."

"I'm falling in love with you, too," he said. Reaching with his left arm around her waist, he pulled her in close and cupped his right hand beneath her cheek. As he tilted her head up to bring her lips to his, the waltz music playing overhead rose with singing violins that matched the soaring of his heart. The soft touch of her kiss sent a thrill throughout his entire body that no experience in his life before or in the future could match. As they broke apart, he touched his forehead lightly down to hers and finally let out his breath as he asked, "Now, for the love of all that is holy, will you please tell me what your real name is?"

Pursing her lips in a mischievous grin that lit her face in a rosy glow, she rolled her eyes playfully and sighed as if relenting. "Fine."

"It's Fanarina, isn't it?"

"And that will be your last guess for the rest of our lives." She shook her head, laughing. "My name is actually just Fanny. Fanny Marie Cunningham."

"You're joking." He squeezed her tightly as though if he held her close enough, he could keep the music of her laughter going forever. "Weren't your parents afraid you would get teased?"

"Well, since my parents were both former dancers turned dance history professors, the idea of naming me after two of the greatest nineteenth-century ballerinas, Fanny Elssler and Marie Taglioni, didn't seem to them like something that should incur mockery," Fanny answered, nestling into his arms with her hands tucked against his chest. "I guess they knew I would end up in the dance world where people would get the reference."

"Sounds like it was your destiny," Law murmured. He kissed her again, longer this time, until she pulled away and bit her lip, pointing her right hand at him.

"You told me once you don't believe in destiny," she said, her voice somehow accusing and enamored in the same breath.

"That, my dear Fanalana," he whispered, catching her hand in his and bringing it to his lips, "was before we met. Because my destiny, well…it had to be you."

EPILOGUE

Six months later

LAW OPENED THE passenger door to his Jeep and held Fanny's hands in his, guiding her out.

"Do I really need to keep this blindfold on?" she complained, stepping out gingerly into the chilly evening air. "I can tell we're at your lot by the length of time and number of turns it took to get here. Us dancers are intuitive that way, you know."

"I like to think I'm included in that 'us dancers' now," he teased, closing the door behind her with one hand and placing the other on the small of her back. "Especially since you and I are preparing to go out on tour as professional dancers in six weeks."

Technically, they were already part of Murray's wedding show tour. They had spent the summer filming short clips of them learning a full first dance as well as demonstrating specific steps and lifts in isolated videos Murray shared on the social media pages of his company's website. Fanny always made sure that she filmed them from the very beginning so that Murray could show all his potential grooms they didn't have to be trained, perfect dancers to perform a graceful first dance with the partner they loved. What really mattered was the love part, and not to toot his own horn, but Law was confident they got that bit just right. At least he hoped so, given what he was about to do when he removed her blindfold.

"Of course you're a dancer, too." She groped the air blindly with her left hand until she found his shirt and wrapped her arm around his waist. "I wouldn't have cast you as Drosselmeyer in *The Nutcracker* if you weren't."

Rehearsing for *The Nutcracker* had definitely not been on his bingo card for that year. Building sets? That, he had been ready for his whole life. He'd had more fun building the wooden Christmas tree that magically grew in size and the candy-themed Kingdom of the Sweets than he could ever remember. It was a good thing his arm was stronger than it had been before the injury, because between the sets, the renovations his general contracting crew was doing on the studio, and finishing the custom-carved welcome sign to the Michael Wright Memorial Football Stadium, he needed all his strength to get through the end of each week. But when Fanny asked him if he would also take on the role of Clara's sorcerer godfather, Herr Drosselmeyer, in her production of *The Nutcracker*, this time he didn't waffle or hesitate even after she showed him the prosthetic nose he would have to wear. His answer was an immediate yes. With Fanny by his side and at the helm of the studio, he knew anything and everything was possible. Together they had even recruited boys from the hockey and basketball teams to join dance classes that fall to help with their agility. Several of them liked it enough to perform in *The Nutcracker*. They called themselves the Ballet Bros and were unapologetic in their newfound love for the art.

"Then I guess you just don't trust me," he sniffed, pretending to get choked up. "Oh, well. We had a good run for the last six months. At least we'll always have Paris."

"You know I trust you—hang on." Fanny wrinkled her nose. "You've never taken me to Paris. Listen if you're going to quote the greatest movie of all time, it has to make sense."

"You're right," he said, moving behind her to untie the blindfold. "We've never been to Paris together. But we have been to Denver at the same time."

As she rubbed her eyes and focused on her surroundings, he pointed to a paving stone directly in front of her, on which he had inscribed the words Denver, Colorado, and the dates they had both been there. She gasped as she took in the line of stones making a pathway flanked by rows of battery-operated candles.

"And Seattle," he said quietly taking her by the hand and leading her along the path, pointing to each stone as he read the inscriptions. "And Tokyo. And Boston. And finally, Crystal Hill."

As they reached the last paver, he pulled her hand to bring her to a tarp covering an object about six inches high and a foot in diameter. He knew the dimensions because he'd carved it himself. Releasing her hand, he knelt to the ground and pulled the cover away.

The object was a perfectly carved log house in miniature, big enough to be a fairly spacious doll's house. It had two floors and was studded in the front with small slate pebbles he had pulled from the stream in the woods. When he flipped a switch on the back, the lights in the tiny house lit up the large windows that fronted the tiny living room.

"Fanny Marie Cunningham," he said, leaning over the house to open the door and pull out a small velvet box. "After years of wandering around, I'm so happy you made your home in Crystal Hill. But even with growing up surrounded by family in this town, I still didn't truly realize how much I belonged here until I found you. You're my home, and if you marry me, I'll build us more than just this house. I'll build us a life."

"Yes." It was her turn to answer without hesitation or second-guessing. "I love you so much, Law."

He placed the ring, a light pink oval morganite surrounded by tiny diamonds the jeweler had called a "ballerina cut," on her left hand, then rose to his feet and swept her up in both his arms and spun her around as she threw her head back and half laughed, half cried with joy. When Law lowered her back to the ground, he swayed her in his arms as the first star twinkled above them like a heavenly disco ball.

"What song are *we* going to use for our first dance?" She looked up at him with love and hope for the future shining in her eyes.

"I don't think we can do any better than 'As Time Goes By,'" he said, humming the tune as he pulled her against his chest, marveling like he did every time at how they fit together as if they were made for one another.

"Okay, but fair warning, I'm going to ask you to play it more than once," she said, misquoting the movie they had watched together at least five times since last May.

"As long as you're dancing with me, I'll play it forever," he said, kissing her like it was the last time, even though he knew both of them were exactly where they were destined to stay. Together.

* * * * *

Harlequin® Reader Service

Enjoyed your book?

Try the perfect subscription for Romance readers and get more great books like this delivered right to your door.

See why over 10+ million readers have tried Harlequin Reader Service.

Start with a Free Welcome Collection with free books and a gift—valued over $20.

Choose any series in print or ebook.
See website for details and order today:

TryReaderService.com/subscriptions